To Rose

Enjoy

Love Val

X

G000163175

WEIRD AND PECULIAR TALES

Paula Harmon and Val Portelli

Publisher: Quirky Unicorn Publications

www.QuirkyUnicornBooks.wordpress.com

Book cover Artist: Paula Harmon
(image credit 'Way to the deep fairy forest' (c) Nadia Forkosh
font: 'CINZEL' from FontSquirrel)

STRANGER FOLK 2

   AT THE BOTTOM OF THE GARDEN 2

   AND THEN 10

   APPEASING THE FAIRIES 19

   NIGHT NAVIGATION 21

   FAIRY DANCE 26

   DUST 29

   RECONDITIONED GOBLINS 33

   MOONLIGHT 37

   THE CHURCHYARD GREMLIN 40

   IN A SPIN 43

   SANTA'S REVENGE 48

   HIDE AND SEEK 51

   TWIG BOY 53

   WHAT HAPPENED TO BUTTERCUP 57

STRANGER BEASTS 61

   VANDA 61

   BAD HOUSEKEEPING 66

   VALENTINE'S DAY LOVE STORY 68

   DEDICATION 71

   A DRAGON IS FOR LIFE 74

A PRIZE 77

DRAGONS' REVENGE 79

PEN FRIENDS 81

GOING HOME 86

TREASURE 91

MERRY THE MERMAID 92

HOW THE DRAGON GOT HIS FLAME 96

HOW THE UNICORN GOT HIS HORN 100

UNDERGROUND CAT 102

THE RHUNICORN 103

TRAVEL RABBIT 105

STRANGER EVENTS 108

FINGERS 108

NEEDLECRAFT 109

HOUSE SHARING 110

AN EMPTY VESSEL 115

HALLOWE'EN CONVERSATION 118

THRESHOLD 120

DREAM WORLD 122

TICKET DUDE 127

THE AUTHOR'S TALE 129

SOFT SOAP 133

THE GRAVEYARD 136

SOMEWHERE ELSE 138

HEALER 141

THE WEDDING GUEST 143

PATIENCE 153

DOOR BELLS 157

DO YOU HAVE ENOUGH TIME? 159

GIGGLES IN THE NIGHT 164

A DRINK AT THE CROWN 171

YE OLDE TAVERN 174

QUIET COMPANY 177

THINGS IN THE NIGHT 180

NIGHT-STALKER 184

ABOUT PAULA HARMON 192

ABOUT VAL PORTELLI 194

STRANGER FOLK

AT THE BOTTOM OF THE GARDEN
Val Portelli

I was looking for a new home when I came across a small village complete with pub, river and Post Office/general store. Mabel, the friendly lady in the Post Office, told me she had the keys to a cottage which was up for sale.

'Mystic Mary,' the previous owner, had died a few weeks before at the grand old age of one hundred and one. She had never married and her only relative was a niece who now lived in Australia and needed to sell the property to receive her inheritance.

The outside of the cottage was chocolate box perfect, although the garden was overgrown and needed some TLC. Inside, although it needed a lot of work I could see the possibilities if it was renovated. It was perfect and I loved it.

The extensive garden was a nightmare. The grass of the lawn was shoulder-high and weeds were everywhere, which made it difficult to see its true potential. Nevertheless, I had already determined that if the price was right this would be my new home.

Two months later the purchase was completed and I moved in. While the builders carried out essential repairs I needed to keep out of their way, so decided to start tackling the garden. It was hard work but eventually I had cut a path through to the end of the property. Moving the debris out of the way I uncovered what appeared to be a rockery.

Intrigued, I delved further into the scrub and was amazed to find a small stream running alongside. Lining both banks was a host of tiny flowers in all colours of the rainbow. Pinks and mauves blended with yellow and blues, purples and whites, all sparkling and shining in the early spring sunshine.

Carefully clearing away some fallen branches I discovered a chain of toadstools, lined up like a row of miniature houses. I was amazed they hadn't been broken by the weight of the undergrowth, but they stood tall and sturdy. Close to the brook was a fallen log which was home to a host of ladybirds. Dusk was now falling, and the setting sun glinted off the fireflies dancing over the water, giving a magical glow to the whole area.

As I prepared for bed that night my attention was caught by lights reflecting off my mirror. With the window fully open I could just see the outline of the rockery and the stream. It was impossible to believe a few insects could be responsible for such an aurora as the whole area was bathed in a gentle coloured light. The next morning the area at the bottom of the garden was brightly lit, but it was nothing more unusual than daybreak.

Perhaps it had only been a dream or my imagination running riot. Whatever it was I donned my gardening gear, and set out to finish the job begun the day before. As I uncovered more of the rockery I could see it was covered with beautiful shells. Getting down on my knees I peered beyond the entrance to the miniature caves inside. It was dim but I could see movement, and assumed it was the home of various small nocturnal creatures.

When my eyes became accustomed to the gloom I saw the fluttering wings of little angels but berating myself for being an imaginative fool I returned to the back-breaking task of clearing the garden. Within a few days the jungle was under control and began to take on the appearance of any normal garden, although I kept the mystical area exactly as it was. Apart from clearing the debris and watering the flowers, my only involvement was to sit on the bench I had installed and watch the activity as night fell.

Spring turned to summer, and with the repairs in the house finished I was able to enjoy every minute of my home. Unless it was pouring with rain, my habit was to go into the garden each evening as the sun went down and watch the activity. One night when it was nearly dark I saw a winged creature fly out and sit on a toadstool preening.

I tried to convince myself it was an insect, but in my heart I knew it was a fairy. Remaining motionless so as not to scare her off, my face broke into a smile as she turned to look at me. She regarded me steadily for a few minutes before, with a flutter of her wings, she took off and disappeared from sight.

After a while I went back into the cottage to try and make sense of what I had seen. The next evening I resumed my previous position on the bench and sat down to wait. For a long while there were only the fireflies dancing over the water, but on the point of giving up I noticed activity in the entrance to the grotto.

Suddenly the one I named Titania appeared, closely followed by a host of other fairies who, taking their lead from her, danced and preened in the gathering dusk. Time passed as I sat enchanted by their antics until I realised it was already dark. I was still able to see them by the moonlight reflecting off their wings, illuminating the area like Chinese lanterns. After that I went down every night at dusk and they accepted my presence without fear. I never mentioned my new friends to anyone; after all who would believe me?

Out of the blue I received a phone call from an old school friend. Actually, Gloria had never been my friend. I remembered her as a nasty, spiteful girl always trying to cause trouble, but somehow she had found out where I lived and wanted me to put her up for the night. Despite my reluctance, she turned up on my doorstep the following evening. To make matters worse she was accompanied by an overweight, vicious cat who immediately tried to scratch my eyes out.

I had always considered myself an animal lover, but this one obviously disliked me as much as I disliked him. As Gloria was the last person I would want to learn my secret I missed my usual trip to the bottom of the garden. Waking early the next morning I found the back door wide open.

'I'm sure I locked it last night,' I told Gloria over breakfast.

'You did,' she replied, 'but Pussykins wanted to go out so I got up in the night to let him out. I must have forgotten to lock up again, but no harm done.'

I was glad to see the back of both of them. As she left she told me I should be thankful Pussykins had caught the bug at the bottom of my garden, but I slammed the door without really listening to her.

Driving to the garden centre the sweet smell of the flowers helped to restore my bad mood. Whilst browsing I came across an area selling garden ornaments and couldn't resist buying a beautiful statue of a tiny angel with outstretched arms. It would look perfect on the rockery, along with the miniature gnome I spied as I headed for the check-out.

The smile back on my face, I headed for home and went straight to the garden to arrange my new treasures. The sun had gone down but I thought it was too early for my fairy friends and intended to come back later to catch up with them. Just as I turned to go indoors I heard a tiny sound and stopped for a moment, perplexed as to what it could be. It sounded like a human voice calling 'Help Me,' but so softly it was at the limit of my hearing. Blaming my imagination, I started walking away but then heard it again, 'Help me.' A flash of colour caught my attention and bending down I saw it was reflecting off something lying in the grass.

It was Titania.

Carefully picking her up I noticed one wing was twisted and lying brokenly at her side. I remembered Gloria's parting comment and was sure that the 'bug' her evil sidekick had caught was my beautiful fairy. A red rage overtook me, but then the practicalities of caring for a fairy with a broken wing set in. Unable to take her to a Doctor or a vet, I gently carried her indoors and made a tiny bed using a cardboard box with some tissues as blankets.

What to do? Feeling silly I opened up my laptop and researched *"How to mend a broken fairy's wing."* Not surprisingly the only answers were about dressing up costumes, but I did find something about broken wings on birds which seemed close enough. Tearing up tiny strips of bandage I approached Titania with the idea of strapping her broken wing against her body to give it a chance to rest and heal.

Carefully picking her up I heard a tiny voice saying 'Thank you.' I had forgotten that she could speak. Was I really losing it? Should I be phoning for the men in white coats to come and get me?

Instead I answered her as quietly as I could. 'I'm going to try to wrap your wing. Tell me if I hurt you.' She seemed to understand me as she turned onto her good side and very carefully I wrapped the bandage securing it under her good wing.

'Are you hungry? I've no idea what fairies eat or drink.'

'We can go without eating but some nectar would help me to heal. Some water or milk would be good too.'

'Would honey be okay?'

'That would be lovely, thank you.'

I knew I had some pure honey in the kitchen and hurried off to get it. As I took the jar out of the cupboard I realised how small she was, and looked around for a suitable dish to serve it. Finally, I picked up two teaspoons, and filling one with honey and the other with milk carried them carefully back to where I had left her.

She sipped at the food and drink then settled back into her bed, and I saw her eyes close as she went off to sleep. This was getting really weird but I decided to leave the spoons close by so she could have some more later if she wanted them.

She stayed with me for two weeks, and I became used to hearing her diminutive voice telling me all about the world she lived in. Several times I changed the bandage until one day she flapped her wings and then flew around the kitchen, perfectly healed. That evening I opened the back door and she blew me a kiss before returning to her own home.

After that I went back to my old routine of going down the garden every night at dusk to visit my fairy friends. They were no longer afraid of me and now appeared as soon as I arrived. Titania must have told them I could be trusted, and I got to know and talk to them all.

*****

This all happened many years ago but I still live in the same cottage. I'm old now and have to use a walking frame to get to the bottom of the garden. I can no longer keep the garden tidy and the weeds and nature have taken over. Soon it will be as it was when I first saw it.

One day I inadvertently let slip to my carer why I was so insistent on going outside, even though it was cold and nearly dark. I still had all my faculties and being able to read upside down when she wrote her report, saw her comment about the onset of mild dementia.

She obviously didn't believe in fairies but I knew better.

I'll leave it to you to judge.

Are these the ramblings of a senile old woman or a true story?

AND THEN
Paula Harmon

And then, she lived happily ever after.

Or did she?

Fast forward twenty years, or maybe a little more. (As they say, the longest ten years of a woman's life are between the ages of forty and sixty.)

Behold Queen Cinderella. She is bored, but doesn't like to say so.

She sometimes looks wistfully at that old ball dress and wonders what happened to her waist. She misses all the petticoats. The frame under her skirts these days is so broad and immobile she has to go sideways through doors. But while wigs are just the place to keep things (like quills and spare change and toothpicks) she misses her hair falling loose and unhindered. She has very firm views about footwear however, and hasn't been able to wear heels since the heir to the throne came along. The glass slippers are on display in the portrait gallery and she blames her bunions on hours of dancing in the wretched things. Everyone thinks the slipper fell off. It didn't. She kicked it off in temper.

The thing about having once been a maid is that you can't help noticing when things aren't done properly. The dusting, the seasoning in the soup, the really terrible darning on her stockings, the state of the brass and silver: poor Cinderella's fingers itch to sort it all out, but it doesn't do to argue with the servants, she knows only too well what sort of revenge they can take. All the same, there is only so much of sitting on a fine cushion sewing a fine seam that a reasonably intelligent woman can take. Dining on strawberries, sugar and cream all day every day for twenty (cough cough) years is definitely the reason why she can't get into that old ball gown anymore.

King Charming is, frankly, an idiot. When they were first married it wasn't so bad, even if he was a bit obsessed with women's feet. Before she got pregnant, once he was happily drooling over other noble-women's shoes she would sneak out of the palace in the dark. In disguise she'd find the places were there was all night dancing and singing but no-one cared what you were wearing or who you were. If she is honest, Cinderella outstrips him on the brains front and would make a much better monarch. Every time he tells her about his decrees, she rolls her eyes. 'Why don't you just order a revolution and save everyone time,' she says.

And then one day, when Cinderella is half-heartedly minding her sparkling sheep on the model farm, a girl in a red cloak pops out of the forest.

The girl says 'sometimes, you just have to go with the flow and then sometimes you have to alter the direction of the flow. The key is to know the difference.' She hands Cinderella a strange device and continues 'if you want to change the way things turned out, twiddle this until you get the date you want to go back to and you can start again. I used it to reboot a wolf. I got him to default to eating sheep instead of people and saved a grandmother. It saved him too. Shall I send him out to eat your flock before it dies of boredom? Anyway, use this wisely and pass it on.

While Cinderella gawps, the girl dashes back into the forest.

For a few seconds, Cinderella stands blinking into the pines, where she can just make out a flash of red. Then she looks at the object in her hand. Nearby, a flunky walks around behind the sheep picking up droppings and another walks around straightening bows. Tonight, there will be a dinner which is supposed to ameliorate the nobles and some of the muttering bourgeoisie. She thinks back to the moment when her whole life changed and then she rewinds time.

*****

The stepmother and ugly stepsisters had gone to the ball crammed into clothes that didn't suit them or fit them and there was Cinderella sitting in the kitchen wondering why there's always a teaspoon in the bottom of the sink after you've finished washing up and whether she'd accidentally put the potato peeler in the bin. Again.

To be honest, she'd given up on the ball idea long ago. She'd tried on the sisters' dresses in secret but otherwise she knew it just wasn't going to happen. Still at least she'd have the evening to herself without people demanding snacks every five minutes. And the kitchen was a lot warmer than the drawing room.

Yes, Cinderella was feeling positive, maybe a little rebellious. She'd considered whether to get the really expensive tea out of the cupboard (the one they'd got from the smugglers to avoid paying duty) and then decided she might as well get the port out instead and top the bottle up afterwards with blackcurrant cordial. She was rummaging around in the bottom of the dresser to get at the good stuff (dislodging the year old dodgy looking bottles of cream liqueur, advocaat and something her more stupid step-sister called peanut colander) when there was a loud explosion. Cinderella jumped and banged her head on the roof of the cupboard.

For a moment she froze, thoughts tumbling through her spinning head: have the stepsisters come back? Is the house being raided? Did I leave something boiling? Does my bum look big in this cupboard? The answer to the last question was yes; but to be fair, Cinderella was wearing a lot of petticoats and her bum was the only thing visible as the rest of her was inside the dresser.

Backing out, she stood up with a frown and found herself face to face with a strange woman who was holding a party dress in exactly the right size, some highly inappropriate shoes which came with a health warning from HM Dept of Chiropody, a pumpkin and some rodents. Like you do.

'Cinderella!' said the woman, brandishing what appeared to be a sparkler, 'I am your Fairy Godmother! You shall go to the ball.'

'Where have you been up to now then?' said Cinderella, 'I've been trapped in this kitchen by my family for ten years.'

'Because this is the pivotal moment when you can meet a handsome prince and live happily ever after!'

'Why couldn't I have had a pivotal moment when I was six so that I got some love and affection and maybe an education and an occasional lie-in?'

Despite going back in time to her youth, Cinderella's feeling of rebellion had not receded. All those years, training up as a domestic instead of as a lady. Why hadn't she just walked away rather than wait for someone to rescue her? After all, she could have been a servant somewhere else and been paid for it; she could have found another career entirely; she could have dressed as a boy and run off to sea or gone to live in the wilds as a wise woman or something.

And then Cinderella realised that the world was her oyster; but that it was up to her to open it in the hope of a pearl rather than a lump of gloop. Even if it was gloop, after ten years of housework, she was used to gloop. She smiled. If the Fairy Godmother had actually been paying attention all these years, she'd have recognised that smile and saved herself a lot of excuses in her annual report.

So, an hour or so later, after Cinderella had boiled up the water for a bath and used the sisters' perfumes, and with some magical assistance had put her hair up and crammed herself into the dress and found a large matching handbag, she watched as the pumpkin and rodents became coach, coachman and horses, and waving goodbye to the Fairy Godmother sped round the corner towards the castle and then stuck her head out of the window and directed the coachman out of the city instead. At the gates, she put on her best pomposity:

'Open the gates immediately!'

The guard warned: 'But it's ten o'clock your..' (under his breath) 'stroppiness..' (louder) 'outside there are....'

'Do you know who I am??'

The gates swung back and the coach barrelled through.

The guard, shutting them again, muttered, 'I know who you are, you're someone who's going to be attacked by highwaymen or wolves. Arrogant...'

The bolts screeched.

But the moon was bright and Cinderella was fine. For two hours the coach sped along, crossing the border before skidding to a halt at the edge of a forest near a small town. A few moments later Cinderella stepped out of the coach, asked the coachman to strip to his underwear, kissed him and patted the horses before they transformed back into their natural state. Carefully placing the ball-dress and crystal shoes into her oversized bag and taking out a blanket, Cinderella put on the coachman's outfit, settled her head on the pumpkin and fell asleep. A rat and four mice curled up on her lap until dawn.

In the morning, Cinderella walked into town and found herself lodgings with an old lady who needed an extra pair of hands and was happy for the first instalment of rent to be paid in pumpkin soup. After that, Cinderella set about selling the ball-dress and starting up a domestic service agency. No woman in her right mind wanted the shoes however. Without any help from anyone, Cinderella found Edward, a young man with brains, married him and expanded her business. As the years passed, she forgot about the crystal shoes and they sat in her coffer under a growing pile of coins with a strange device, the purpose of which was now a blur.

One evening, Edward said over dinner, 'those dwarves in the forest are after crystals. Not sure if the diamond mine's run out or they just want a sideline for the financially challenged. Shame we haven't got any to sell.'

The next day, Cinderella headed into the trees with the slippers in a nap-sack. It was a long way through the undergrowth to the cottage but every time she thought she was lost, a group of mice squeaked at her till she changed direction. They looked like mice she'd once known, but that was ridiculous. The cottage was in a clearing. She had heard dire things about the state of it and was anticipating filth and chaos, but when she arrived there was a girl standing outside under sparkling windows, putting clothes through a mangle and singing to an audience of wildlife.

'Hello,' said Cinderella. The girl looked up and stopped singing. Her hair was black as ebony, her skin as white as snow (which was hardly surprising since there wasn't much sunlight getting through the trees) and her lips were as red as blood. It was a bit unnerving to look at her.

'I'm Cinderella. I've got some crystal to sell to the dwarves.'

'I'm Snow White,' said the girl, 'I'll call them.'

She shrieked into the trees, and after patting all the animals went back to the mangle, grimacing as she wound the handle.

'I hate housework,' she said, 'All I want to do is run a wildlife rescue centre. I don't know how I ended up here. One minute I was being trained up to a future of idle luxury, eating strawberries and cream. I knew they'd marry me off and I'd be pregnant every year and I was thinking how boring it all sounded. Then I hit sixteen. Instead of having someone marching me down the aisle, someone dragged me into the woods to kill me quickly with a dagger. As if that's not bad enough, he then wimped out and sent me into the forest so wolves or starvation or cold could kill me off much slower and more painfully. Then when I thought I'd found some men to save me, it turns out they live in such a mess they can't find their own er... anyway, I can't live in that kind of chaos so I found myself cleaning up and waiting for a handsome prince to whisk me off to a life of idle luxury, eating strawberries and cream and being pregnant every year. Is it me? Only it still doesn't seem like much of a life, does it? Where did I go wrong? Anyway, while we're waiting, let's have a look at the crystals.'

Cinderella pulled the slippers out of the knapsack and a strange device fell onto the ground. She picked it up and turned it over in her hand, frowning, remembering.

'These are pretty,' said Snow White, holding a slipper against her foot then handing it back, 'but they look dead uncomfortable.' She pointed at the device. 'What's that?'

Cinderella remembered a flash of red and said words which came out of her dim memory, 'sometimes, you just have to go with the flow and then sometimes you have to alter the direction of the flow. The key is to know the difference. If you want to change the way things turned out, twiddle this until you get the date you want to go back to, and you can start again.'

Snow White looked at the laundry and back at the cottage. 'How will they manage without me though? I'm very fond of them really.'

'I run an agency that supplies domestic service. I'm sure I can sort something out for them,' said Cinderella. 'Anyway, use this wisely and pass it on.'

Cinderella passed over the device. Snow White took it. Her eyes sparkled as she twiddled with the time-turner and disappeared. The animals scattered.

Cinderella was left on her own with the laundry in the clearing. After a few moments, seven dwarves rounded the cottage and fourteen eyes sized up the value of the slippers.

'Hello lads,' said Cinderella, 'I've got a business proposition.'

And then they all lived happily ever after. Probably.

APPEASING THE FAIRIES
Val Portelli

We'd lived in the house for a while now, and "She who must be obeyed" had started hinting about bringing it up to date. First she wanted a new bathroom, so every spare minute between slaving to earn a crust I hacked at age-stuck tiles and crumbling plaster.

'I'm trying to work here. Can you keep the noise down? How can I have a bath when it's full of debris?' were my only supportive comments.

Finally it was done and peace resumed. We were both happy with the result and things returned to normal. Not for long.

'That old shed at the bottom of the garden is an eyesore. Have you seen these beautiful summer houses? There's a sale on at the moment; such good value. Look at this one. It would be perfect for that corner of the garden.'

In the fifteen years we had been married this was the first time I had felt wary about my origins. When we first met I told her I was an orphan, and all our family photos had been destroyed in a fire. She accepted my story, and although over the years we had argued about the shed, it was the normal bickering of a married couple.

What started off as a joke became a bone of contention between us. As I had kept the secret all these years it was too late now to admit I wasn't just being awkward. There was a real reason behind my adamant refusal to demolish the shed.

I waited until she was enjoying the luxury of a bubble bath in our perfect bathroom before venturing down to the end of the garden to get advice.

'So, in effect you're saying you are giving us a month's notice,' Oberon challenged.

'No, I don't mean it like that,' I tentatively replied. 'I just came here to ask for suggestions. Since I was made semi-mortal I've lost the fairy instinct. How can I sort out this problem without upsetting my wife even more?'

'Just put your foot down,' Oberon responded. 'She's a female and obliged to do as her superior demands.'

Suddenly a female voice interjected. 'Stop your wittering Oberon and get the suitcases down from the top toadstools. I've been saying for ages this shed needs updating. We can go and stay with my mother for a few weeks and come back when the new building is finished. Fairy gossamer blue curtains will look perfect. Just insist on that and we'll be back as soon as it's habitable,' Aurora instructed me.

'Trust the females to solve a problem,' I thought, as I went in to tell my wife the good news.

NIGHT NAVIGATION
Paula Harmon

Driving around without a map at weekends was Sean and Nicole's thing. They liked to follow the road randomly, following signs for odd place names, stopping for stale crisps in strange little pubs where yokels looked sideways at them. Lanes could lead nowhere or to soulless hamlets comprising of nothing but holiday lets or they could suddenly join a main road heading into a busy tourist resort. Sean and Nicole discovered tiny coves and ribbon bestrewn trees; the glint of sea to the south, mild or furious; the lushness of farmland to the north, undulating over the outlines of hill fort terraces and diving into ripe valleys.

By sunset they holed up in what passed for civilisation, eating in buzzing restaurants, clubbing if they felt like it, eventually snug in their own weekend flat overlooking the bay.

It was always Sean who drove. Nicole was lookout, spotting silly place names, pointing out the locals.

Tonight was the first time she had driven here at all. And it was dark. And she drove blinded with tears.

He shouldn't have done that.

It was miles before she could see properly. Even clear eyed, all she saw in front of her was their argument playing over and over. All she could hear were the words.

He shouldn't have said that.

The roads twisted in the darkness under trees and up over the downland. Bend after hollow way after turn after hill after valley.

You need to stop.

Nicole pulled up, got out of the car and suddenly nauseous, vomited into the verge.

After a while, she found something to clean her face. Her hands shook and she wiped them down her jacket, down the legs of her jeans.

Stop thinking about it.

Nicole felt an unease crawling up her spine. She was suddenly aware of the antiquity of the land. All land is ancient, but some land has never forgotten it. She did not know where she was. She went to reach into the car for her phone to find out, but she felt uncertain of making any movement, even turning round. Especially turning round.

You're lost.

Were the steep cliffs and the rolling sea over the hill to her left or right? The night's clouded blackness was sucking at her, but Nicole knew if she could will herself to get back into her car and drive, she would eventually find ... somewhere.

On either side the land rose in defensive ridges. Cold air rolled down them and Nicole, hugging her jacket around her, forced herself to look properly. She was being ridiculous. They were just hills, it was just a road. Nowhere is far from anywhere and the car's tank was full. It was just that the argument was still flashing through her mind. Reiterated vicious words interrupted her ability to think, to try and recognise something.

Why are you on your own?

Shh - I need to concentrate.

Slowly, Nicole made herself turn around. Behind her the road curved away into invisibility. She had stopped near a small grove. A few leaning stones, smoothed by time and innumerable hands, were mantled by an oak while yews stood guard on either side. There was barely enough light to make it out but it was vaguely familiar. In daylight it had had a primitive charm. She and Sean had fooled around it, pretending to push the stones over and stage-whispering nonsense had acted out a sacrifice... She had lain down in that dark centre and Sean had pretended....

Was that only today?

No, yesterday. It's later than you think.

Nicole looked at her barely visible sweating hands and wiped them down her jeans again. Her thoughts became more insistent.

He shouldn't have said that. He shouldn't have done that.

What are you going to do now?

She rubbed her eyes and shook her head. She had to keep moving. As Nicole turned back to the car, there was a flicker. Had she been here so long with the lights on and the door open that the battery was draining? She hesitated, but the beam of the headlights and the glow of the interior remained steady. A fox must had run across. Or something. Instinctively she opened the passenger's door, ready for Sean to ask her what had taken her so long and then she saw her bag on the seat and remembered.

You could stay here.

Why would even the notion of remaining in this place cross her mind? Why was she talking to herself?

*You **should** stay here.*

The lights flickered again and this time she was watching. Not a fox. A person, people. They were walking towards her and she wanted to turn back, sweat chilling on her face, but could not move. Her thoughts became louder.

Look round, we're waiting.

They were not her thoughts. Had any of them been her thoughts? She turned and saw them: more people emerging from the grove.

You were here yesterday. You mocked us. You pretended to draw blood yet left the ground thirsty.

'We didn't mean to make fun of anyone, we didn't know anyone was watching,' Nicole argued weakly. But wasn't that when the argument started? Hadn't that been when their mood soured?

The people had not moved but seemed to be pressing in on her. She reached for her pocket, and stopped. Appalled at herself, she balled her right hand tightly instead.

We know what you've got.

'It was ...' she started.

It was what? It has been in your heart for a long time. We just showed it to you.

'If you want blood,' Nicole said, reaching into her pocket again, 'here….' and threw the knife into the centre of the stone circle. She was shaking uncontrollably, tears ran down her face and soaked the collar of her stained jacket.

The people were coming closer, herding her into the grove. One leaned in and stared intently. All Nicole could register were the eyes: no whites, no iris. Voids. The soft cold voice burned in her head:

You will stay here. It said. **His** *blood is not enough. Now we need yours.*

FAIRY DANCE
Val Portelli

People can be dense sometimes; you'd think they could at least recognise cautionary road signs.

Anastasia was adamant we posted sufficient warning well before the 'Day of the Dance.' Every fairy remembered the horrors of a few years previously when so many of our number were ploughed down by reckless drivers with no thought for the little folk.

Although we had been in existence for more years than all their ancestors, there were still those who didn't believe in us. It was left to the young children and the old ones to have the sight; the others were too full of their own importance. Their lives only consisted of apps and social media, which was a strange way of communicating with their fellow beings.

This was our biggest night of the year, and despite the non-believers it was important we kept the magic alive. Preparations had been ongoing for months, the circles prepared, wings polished and the rowan trees trimmed to look their best.

Various meetings had been held. We had even invited the wizards and witches to give their advice on the best way to manage crowd control, and asked the goblins for ways to develop the publicity aspects.

Most of their thoughts were too dark to be entertained, but we did gain some useful insights. Rumblings developed amongst our lower ranks. They were accustomed to spending their lives in joy and frivolity, not compiling spreadsheets and trying to charm publicity agents into marketing the big event.

In the old days we flew over to speak to each other face to face. Word spread throughout the kingdom without the involvement of the ether or sending reminders if a computer crashed. We had done the best we could. The number of online acceptances received would make this our best year ever if everyone turned up.

The big day arrived, the excitement grew and there was more fluttering than usual as we prepared to greet our guests. As dusk fell the musicians warmed up and the sweet sound of fairy pipes began to fill the arena. The tables were groaning under the weight of honey, milk, berries, mushrooms, nectar and nuts, ready to refresh the dancers.

We waited and waited. Time passed and no one arrived. All our efforts had gone to waste, but surely at least a few should have turned up for this momentous occasion.

Anastasia was as angry as I had ever seen her, even though she was renowned for her bad temper.

She stomped off to the perimeters to speak to the bouncers and find out if they had actually seen any guests.

I wouldn't like to be in the shoes or the wings of the fairy who suggested we employ trolls to control entry.

Not only had they kept the humans out, they had frightened all the fairies away.

Oh well, there's always next year.

DUST
Paula Harmon

I was clearing out my wardrobe when I saw him. He
was clothed in quite a neat little outfit evidently made
from bits of my stash of dressmaking fabric which was
spilling out all over the place. The stash itself was
tangled up with shoes I'd never wear again, random bits
of writing shoved out of the way in haste, two old
handbags, a set of broken straighteners (the ones which
accidentally got a carrier bag melted onto them) and a
slinky dress which had slipped off the hanger
(presumably to avoid being forced over my less than
slender figure, thereby ruining its straight lines, since I
haven't got any). He was standing pressed against the
wooden back of the wardrobe defending himself with a
shield made out of an old loyalty card and waving a
forgotten mascara wand like a sword. He looked
terrified.

'Hello' I said. After all, what else does one say
when one sees a six-inch mystical creature in the back
of the wardrobe.

'Put your weapon down or... or else!' he said.

I realised I was holding the thin thingy
attachment for the vacuum cleaner.

'OK' I said, 'I'll put down the nozzle if you put
down the mascara and tell me what you are.'

I did as I'd promised and sat in what I hoped
was a non-threatening stance. After a moment's
hesitation, the creature put down his defensive weapons

and quivering a little, waved his arms to show me the back of the wardrobe.

'I can't help,' he said, 'I can't find the door to Narnia either.'

'It's not in here,' I said sadly, 'I've looked often enough. On the other side of that wall is the airing cupboard.'

The creature looked even more scared. 'Not the airing cupboard!' he squeaked. 'I don't want to mess with the laundry fairies, they swear like fishwives and have biceps bigger than their heads.'

'There are laundry fairies?' I said with some annoyance. 'I hadn't noticed.'

'They're not helpers. They're pixies. Have you got a lot of odd socks?'

'Oh' I said, 'But then who are you?'

The creature stood up straighter and announced: 'I'm ÆLFNOÐ' then added apologetically, 'It means 'bold elf.' I'm a brownie.'

I thought about this for a bit. Weren't brownies the ones who help around the house, who do all the chores which the exhausted housewife can't manage?

'I hadn't realised I had a brownie, it's not been obvious.'

ÆLFNOÐ shuffled his feet. 'I hate housework' he mumbled. 'It's not a proper elf job. Pixies and sprites get to have fun. Brownies just get to clean things up ready for people to mess them up again and what thanks do you get?'

'Tell me about it,' I said.

'And I'm frightened to go out because if I meet the laundry fairies I'm liable to find myself inside a sock inside a random pillow case and shoved in a corner of the airing cupboard. All I want is some peace and quiet and a home of my own to look after.' I patted him gently as he started to sob.

I thought about it for a bit and told him not go anywhere for a moment and not to be frightened. I passed him a magazine to calm his nerves.

I got the loft ladder down as quietly as possible and moved some things about. Our attic is quite nice, with a window in the gable end. If we actually cleared out the accumulations of many years of family life, it could make a nice room.

After about half an hour I opened the wardrobe door, to find ÆLFNOÐ intently reading up on the latest interior design trends, and held a basket out to him. 'Trust me for a moment and jump in here.'

He hesitated, but I said he could take the magazine and some bits from my craft stash and the mascara wand and this was how I took him up into the attic. My daughter's abandoned dolls house was now near the window and I had put a piece of ribbon across the front door. I handed ÆLFNOÐ some craft scissors and told him to make himself at home.

We toasted his new life with some tiny glasses of wine and I sat there in the light of the window, listening to him clattering about inside the dolls house, reorganising things, and thought that if I could get a table and chair up here, I would have somewhere quiet to write away from the family and could keep ÆLFNOÐ company.

Then I left him to it. I raised the ladder and closed the loft. I shoved everything back into the bottom of my wardrobe, opened the door of the airing cupboard and told any laundry fairies who might be lurking invisibly what I'd do to them if I ever caught them.

Then I went downstairs to finish the wine.

Perhaps I should try and be a better housewife. Or maybe I could contribute to research into dust inhalation to find out exactly how much is needed to make one hallucinate. Or maybe I really do have a house infested with elves.

It would explain a lot.

RECONDITIONED GOBLINS
Val Portelli

'I'm not fat,' Petunia said indignantly. 'I'm just a bit short for my weight. If I was seven feet instead of four feet three I'd be perfect. Anyway, you can't talk. With a belly like that you'd give Father Christmas a run for his money, and as for that little rotund specimen you call a friend…'

Nag, nag, nag. That's all she seemed to do these days. What had happened to the willowy beauty who had bewitched him all those years ago? Igor had warned him she would turn into an old hag like her mother, but he had been besotted. Anyway, his friend was in the same boat, he had married Lilywhite, Petunia's sister who could nag for fairyland.

'I'm just taking the dinosaur for some exercise,' he called as he made for the door.

'Don't give me that. I know you're off to The Toadstool to try out that new imported mead, and no doubt you'll be ogling that barmaid who's no better than she ought to be. Mother warned me but I was a fool and didn't listen, and now see what I have to put up with. I should have taken her advice and married Elfin, at least he knows how to treat a lady. And he always gets invites to the best fairy balls, not that I would go with you anyway, showing me up with that ridiculous green cap with the bells on.'

With the shrill screech of his wife's voice still ringing in his ears Gumbor escaped, dragging Dino behind him. She was right about one thing though; he had arranged to meet Igor in the pub and had heard the new barmaid was a comely wench.

After a brief tussle with Dino who wanted to chase the exciting dragon smells, Gumbor managed to tie the animal up to the post, kept for that purpose at the rear of his favourite drinking haunt. Or at least it used to be. What had happened to the rickety old benches, and the curtains so full of dust if you sneezed you would immediately grant the nearest human three wishes? The peeling paintwork and gloomy corners had been replaced by plush sofas, cream and maroon walls and disco style strobe lights illuminating the bunny waitresses with their skimpy costumes and bobbly tails.

'Over here, Gum,' he heard a voice call from behind the gazebo.

'What have they done to the place Ig?' he asked his fat friend.

'Didn't you read the Faerie Herald? It's been taken over by that foreign conglomerate. They've got all new fancy barmaids and they won't let you in unless you're wearing your Sunday best. They've stopped selling Goblin slurp and even the food is bits on sticks, nothing like a good old-fashioned gut-buster. What are we going to do?'

Gumbor was in despair. Scrambling up onto the window ledge he peered through the sparkling windows and his eyes nearly popped out when he saw the voluptuous wench behind the bar. She was everything a Goblin could desire. Looking down at himself he remembered the dashing, handsome beast he used to be, and determined to do something about it.

Making his way home he found a note from his wife, 'Gone to stay with Mother for a month. Make your own dinner for a change.' So he did. At first it was a disaster, but gradually he learnt how to fix himself proper, healthy food. He started taking care of his clothes and even bought new ones. He set himself on an exercise regime, lost weight, took daily baths and gradually saw the old Gumbor re-emerge from the remnants of the fat, scruffy goblin he had become.

Igor had joined him in his endeavours, and four weeks later the two friends looked at each other and pronounced themselves fit to brave the New Toadstool for the first time. With a high-five and a jaunt in their steps they pushed open the doors and made their entrance. Female eyes swivelled in their direction, showing nothing but admiration for these two impressive goblins no one recognised.

Ordering themselves reduced-fat honey meads they found a quiet corner and sat down to peruse the other clientele. Although there were plenty of good looking females, Igor and Gumbor found themselves attracted to two particularly beautiful specimens on a nearby table who were casting "come hither" glances in their direction.

'Wow, the shorter one is really something,' Gumbor whispered to his friend.

'I prefer the other one,' Igor whispered back. 'Shall we invite them over for a drink?' So they did.

The evening passed in delightful company and it was only as the clock struck midnight, and they invited the girls back to their respective homes that they thought to ask their names.

'Don't you recognise us?' asked Gumbor's lady friend. 'My name is Petunia, and this is my sister Lilywhite. The fee for that witches' potion was worth every penny to get our men back.'

And they all lived happily ever after.

MOONLIGHT
Paula Harmon

In the middle of the night Madge woke. She didn't know why.

They had been in the holiday bungalow for several days now. After months of stress and exhaustion, they slept like logs. But tonight she woke and sat up in bed, illuminated by the moonlight coming through the patio doors.

'Fat goblins at midnight,' she said.

'Who are you calling fat?' said Derek, startled, 'and it's gone midnight.'

'It was just what came to mind. I don't know why.'

Somewhere outside, something squeaked.

Madge went to fill their water glasses.

As she came back, she saw Derek fiddling with the patio door.

'It's a bit dark to go outside isn't it?' she said.

'I'm not,' he answered, 'I'd forgotten to lock it.'

'I don't know why you're worried,' said Madge, 'we're in the middle of nowhere.'

Derek, snuggling up to her, shrugged and started snoring.

Madge, cuddled into him and, after a few seconds, started snoring too.

Outside, a small rotund figure kicked the patio door-frame in irritation. Behind it, in the shadow of the veranda, two other small rotund figures glowered at an even smaller one, mounted on something which was fidgeting on feathered feet.

'Had to be clever, didn't you, Blorc?'

'Sorry Da... I mean Sir, I just thought it was a good idea.'

'All we had to do was creep in. Oddlin had done the telepathic doodah so they didn't lock up. All we needed was for Ningle to stand on his shoulders and open the door so we could get inside and nick their treasures.'

Blorc's mount reared and gripping hold of the mane tighter, he argued: 'Yeah but Da... I mean Sir... Zobbly said it's no good. Their lot did some raids last week and found it was a waste of time. They don't keep treasure, humans. Not nowadays. Least not the sort you can melt down and sell to the dwarves. It's all gadgets nowadays. Zobbly's lot say the dwarves won't take 'em till they know how to use 'em. We'd need the humans to show us. I thought we could scare 'em up a bit.'

'So you telepath an image of a goblin raiding party!'

'Well, yeah.'

'We're quarter the size of the female, and she's that short, she wouldn't be able to get on some of the rides at the funfair. How could four of us frighten them?'

'Ah, well, that's where the secret weapon comes in!'

Blorc patted his mount. The rest of the goblins glared at it as they turned to go, shifting their empty swag bags over sloping shoulders as they walked out into the moonlight, muttering under their breath.

'Blorc, son, that thing's about as scary as a powder puff stuffed with needles.'

Under the full moon, the mount reared again and let out a strangled woof. It sounded as if someone had sat heavily on a squeaker toy. A pungent smell wafted from its exterior and attracted by it, the mosquitoes homed in, piercing the goblins' chain mail.

'Thing is, Blorc,' sighed his father, 'when you're going to make a hybrid, you cross a werewolf with something bigger than a chihuahua.'

'Yeah but Da... sir...' Blorc gave up. The older generation never tried anything new.

He patted the werehuahua and turned it for home.

From his saddleback, he pulled out Madge's mobile, which she'd left on the veranda table and started fiddling. Hey! A mirror! He grinned at himself and pressed another button, to be temporarily blinded. Then he saw that his image had been magically transposed onto the gadget.

Dad was a fool. Wait till he showed the dwarves, he could start a whole new enterprise.

THE CHURCHYARD GREMLIN
Val Portelli

As usual I got the blame for the break down, just because my surname was Goblin. It didn't help that my parents had named me Gus, so obviously everyone called me Gus the Gremlin.

With my big nose, spindly frame and one leg longer than the other I had a hard time at school. It was even worse when I started work as a mechanical engineer; every time something went wrong I was the scapegoat. I'm sure most problems were caused by people being careless, knowing they could pass the buck and get off scot-free by blaming me.

When it became too much I moved on, but my reputation followed me. I'd only been in this job a few weeks but already my nickname was Jonah. We were about halfway to our destination, six of us in the van, driving along in the middle of nowhere when it spluttered and came to a halt.

With the dense surrounding forest the mobiles couldn't get a signal, and even the Satnav had packed up. 'We should never have brought him with us,' I heard the grumbling from the front of the van. 'Might have known something would go wrong,' another of the lads muttered, looking in my direction.

I couldn't decide whether to get angry or just keep my head down, but as we all got out to peruse our surroundings I glanced at the petrol gauge beyond the driver's open door. 'Perhaps it might have been an idea to top up the tank before we set off,' I remarked.

Sick of the lot of them I wandered off a few yards, and from my new viewpoint saw what looked to be an Esso logo blinking in the distance.

'That looks like a garage,' I said pointing. 'Do we have such a thing as a petrol-can, or is that my fault too?' Looking rather red-faced one of the guys handed me a container, and without another word I set off over the fields. It was getting dark, and after about ten minutes walking I regretted not asking one of the others to keep me company.

Climbing a gate set in a hedge I was spooked when I found myself in a graveyard, with an ancient church looming in the darkness beyond. Determined to reach my destination I continued my journey through the monuments, and had nearly made the other side when in the distance I saw a shadowy figure emerge.

Scared out of my wits I climbed the nearest tree quicker than I would have believed possible. The branches provided little cover, and I watched in horror as a light flashed at irregular intervals and the creature came closer to my hiding place.

A sudden flash blinded me as a disembodied voice called up 'Hello, up there. Are you OK? Sorry if I startled you. I was taking some photos and thought you were a tree gremlin or something. I'm Linda by the way.'

Feeling like an idiot I quickly climbed down to greet the lady standing below. She was holding a camera in one hand, which was noticeably smaller than the other.

'Nice to meet you Linda,' I said as we shook hands. 'I'm Gus, but you can call me Gremlin.'

'I'm Miss Lew. You can call me Loopy,' she said with a smile.

Somehow I had the feeling we were made for each other.

IN A SPIN
Paula Harmon

It was Saturday.

My husband had taken the children out on their paper round.

Monday to Friday, I work in an office, assessing risk, writing reports and meeting targets instead of being creative. All week, the housework piles up. Recently, it had been piling up for a month. On that Saturday, I needed to get a grip.

One day, I thought, if I ever finish my novel, I might get rich and famous. Then I can write all day and hire staff to do the boring stuff.

I only needed to write twenty thousand more words and I'd be finished. Then…who knew what the future might hold.

But on that Saturday, the novel had to wait.

The house was quiet but I mustn't get side-tracked. There were chores to be done before I could write.

I went to the laundry bin. It was empty. How wonderful, the children were playing hide and seek with their dirty clothes again. Well, mostly seek. Not much effort had gone into hiding things; dirty clothes were simply scattered across the children's bedroom floors.

My fingers itched. If I just typed a few words it couldn't hurt. Putting down the laundry, I opened up the laptop and started to write.

At the edge of my hearing, came a tiny chuckle and my vision was obscured by sparkling lights. I blinked.

'Naughty, naughty,' said the laptop and slammed itself shut, nearly severing my fingers. Imagining things is what I'm good at. But this was a little too much.

Shaking a little, I put the laptop aside and went back to the housework. I needed to find all the dirty crockery and glasses hidden around the childrens' beds and desks. As I approached their rooms, I heard a clatter and some giggling. How very odd.

I entered my daughter's room and saw the plates running away by themselves, rolling under the desk to snigger and hide in discarded homework. This was not normal, even for our house. It took me half an hour to round them up and force them, struggling, into the dishwasher. I wondered if I should ask for a day's leave.

Not for the first time, I wondered how one small family could be so chaotic. Housework is such a depressing exercise. The place would look lovely when I finished...for all of five minutes.

I reached for the vacuum cleaner but it turned its back on me. I could hear it mumbling.

'What's wrong?' I said before I could stop myself.

'You haven't bothered with me for a month,' muttered the vacuum cleaner, 'you prefer that rotten old laptop.'

I couldn't really deny this. I patted the vacuum but he wouldn't make friends.

'I'm sick of eating spiders,' he said. 'I want to work for a PROPER housewife.'

'Well, all you've got is me,' I said and bumped him up the stairs, ignoring his complaints.

I managed to finish my chores before the family got home. I had perhaps an hour of peace to write in. But the laptop wouldn't open. Every time I tried, it snarled and snapped at me.

'Whatever is going on?' I said aloud.

I heard another chuckle. It was coming from inside the airing cupboard. I waited outside for a second and then wrenched the door open.

Inside was a laundry fairy, balanced on top of the piles and piles of clean clothes which had been accumulating for weeks while I wrote my novel. It was a precarious perch because the whole family, instead of putting their clothes away without being asked, just rummaged from time to time.

'Serves you right,' said the laundry fairy. She was hefty (for an elf) and muscly. A clothes peg and odd sock were tattooed on each bicep. 'You haven't been doing your chores,' she sneered, 'it's no fun losing your socks when you're such a terrible housewife anyway. So I put a spell on everything.'

'Well, you can pack it in!' I said. 'I am not a big woman, but I am bigger than a laundry fairy.' I wrestled her off the clean clothes and bundled her up with the dirty ones. I'm telling you, those wings look flimsy but they're sharp as razors. I took the whole squirming bundle to the washing machine.

'Yum yum,' said the washing machine, 'I thought you'd never feed me!'

'And you can shut up too, you gluttonous pig, I fed you three times on Wednesday!' I snapped.

I shoved everything inside, put in extra stain remover and turned it on.

All the household goods stopped chuckling and the sparkling lights went out. I could just make out the furious face of the laundry fairy as she rotated inside the machine, covered in soap suds. She was shaking her fist but I didn't care. I stuck my tongue out.

When the family came home they found me locked in the spare room typing. I had only managed to write twenty words of my novel and was having a little cry. But at least the laptop had returned to normal.

My husband said, 'did you know you've washed the reds with the blues and now everything is purple? And how many times have I told you not to put an underwired bra in the machine? Now there's a funny knocking noise coming from inside even though the cycle has finished. It sounds almost,' he said, with a chuckle, 'as if someone small and angry is trapped inside.'

I glared at him and then glanced out of the window. In our overgrown garden, something small and green was creeping up on the shed with a wand in its hand.

'Haven't you got stuff to do outside?' I asked, getting up to peg the laundry fairy on the line until she was sorry.

'Oh I don't know if I can be bothered,' my husband answered, 'maybe the garden elves will do it for me.'

'I wouldn't take the risk if I were you,' I said, 'I really wouldn't.'

SANTA'S REVENGE
Val Portelli

The pixies were not happy. Just because some silly humans had upset Santa they had been given more jobs to do when they should have been on holiday.

Everyone knew that by the 12th day of Christmas the decorations had come down, the tree had been taken to the tip, and there would be no more turkey sandwiches, turkey curry, cold turkey with pickles, turkey soup or turkey vol au vents, at least until next year.

Then they were free to pack their spare wings and fly off to somewhere warm until the Spring.

At the meeting Father Christmas was still angry and wouldn't listen to anyone's complaints. 'If we don't nip this in the bud now, the naughty list for 2019 will be out of control,' he shouted.

'Harry, you're in charge of advertising for new franchisees. You can start by setting up a Facebook page, and making lots of new friends. Here's a list of people who are definitely NOT to be included.

'Stella, here's a photocopy of the same names. I want you to get the factory working again to organise some extra presents for them this year.'

'But Santa,' the fairy gasped in amazement, 'these are the ones on the super naughty list. Why are they getting extra presents? A football and pliers for Hrick, pincers and a Christmas sack for Van, the matriarch help fairy for Fichael, socks for Veberley, sticky tape and a scarf for Valpor, writing paper and sparkly things for Laupa. There are even group train tickets to Battsea and a stay in a large cottage in the Forest for all of them. I don't understand.'

'I'll explain,' Santa grinned evilly.

'Even though the fairy is old and ugly she will sit on Fichael's shoulder for the forthcoming year, and hiss in his ear until he has to believe in her.

'There will be over a thousand socks for Veberley, which she will have to spend the year sorting into pairs. That will keep her busy until next Christmas when she will discover there are 23 left over that don't match.

'Hrick will spend his year playing football. The rest of his team will be lovely young ladies in long red stockings, but every time he tries to kick the ball it will stay magically an inch out of reach. Instead of a net, the goal will be covered with Christmas tree lights which he will have to untangle with the pliers before he can score.

'Van's sack used to belong to the coalman and will be filled with turkeys. It's his job to use the pliers to remove every speck of dust from their feathers until they all glow in the dark again.

'Valpor will have to use the sticky tape to keep putting back the skin the zombies bite off her, and the scarf is to protect her neck so she doesn't become one of them. She doesn't get off that easily.

'Laupa will use the sparkly things to illustrate the stories she writes on the paper. What she won't know is that the paper is magic and will automatically delete every story as soon as it is finished.'

'That should keep them out of mischief,' Stella smiled, happy they would all get their comeuppance.

'But what about the trip to London and the holiday?' Harry asked.

'Ah' said Santa, 'that's the best bit. The Rottweilers and the kittens, which are in fact fast-growing tigers with claws like knives, will go with them to the cottage. The wild, teenage ponies are staying there too, and are already bad-tempered being cooped up with nothing to do.

'Oh yes, I forgot. You'd better throw in some shovels and air-freshener as well. You wouldn't believe how smelly a cottage can get with reindeer that have eaten too many sprouts, especially when they only moved out a few days ago.

'If that doesn't work I'll set the gremlins on them. Now let me have some peace so I can see what's happening on Facebook.'

HIDE AND SEEK
Paula Harmon

Sam covered his face with his hands and turned to the tallest wall 'one…two..three…'

Jane and I scattered, stifling our giggles. 'Ten…eleven..twelve…'

I saw Jane turn a corner and lost sight of her. The ruins were a maze. I clambered over a low wall and ducked down. 'Thirty-three….thirty-four…thirty-five…'

I was in a square space. Walls on all four sides made of grey blocks, a small gap in one wall – maybe it had been a doorway. 'Fifty-six…fifty-seven…fifty-eight…'

It must have been a home once. That's what Mum said – this was once a small settlement. Impossible to imagine now, just squares laid out with low walls, nothing inside them, nothing to make them more alive than a lego project.

'Seventy-nine…eighty…eighty-one…'

I traced my finger on the damp stone. There was lichen and maybe a fossil. Dad said there would be fossils. I tried to squint. My knees were getting damp on the wet ground and I shifted so that I was squatting instead, without raising my head above the top of what was left of the wall. 'Eighty-eight, eighty-nine…ninety…'

What would our house look like if all that was left was a metre of wall and everything that made it

51

home had been taken out? I closed my eyes and tried to imagine. 'Ninety-three…ninety-four…ninety-five.'

I must be getting used to the cold, or maybe the wind had changed direction. I wasn't as cold anymore and the draught had gone, there even seemed to be heat coming from somewhere. 'Ninety-six…ninety-seven…ninety-eight…'

I opened my eyes. There was a tiny horse carved out of something by my feet, lit by the light of flames. I picked it up and got to my feet, confused. The space around me was dark. A fire was burning in the middle of it. The walls were high and the only light came from a gap in the high roof and the low doorway. Pots and wooden furniture were tidily placed around the room.

I could hear people talking close by but Sam's voice seemed further away. 'Ninety-nine….One Hundred… Coming – Ready or….'

Clasping the tiny horse, I rushed to the doorway and ran outside. There were no ruins: I was surrounded by buildings and strangers in strange clothes were everywhere. One of them turned and stared at me. Pointed. Called out with words I didn't know.

And I couldn't hear Sam anymore.

TWIG BOY
Val Portelli

I was happiest on my own, away from the mockery of
the town's folk.

    'Hey Twig-boy. Have you got any sticks?'

    'Or stones? Here, have some of mine.'

    I flinched as the hail of rocks narrowly missed
me but didn't dare retaliate. As usual, there were five or
six in the gang who were intent on making my life even
more miserable than it was already. Leaning heavily on
my cane I scuttled away into the haven of the
countryside where I could hope to find some peace.

    Eventually I reached the top of the hill, and
settling against a tree trunk listened as the birds sang
their goodnights. Amidst all the beautiful music a
painful cry reached my ears. A forlorn pair of eyes
gazed from beneath the bushes, its tiny whimpers
appealing to me to heal his pain. As I reached to lift
him up he cowered away, quivering in fright. My voice
seemed to reassure him, allowing me to wrap my jacket
round him to restore some warmth while I gently
examined his damaged leg.

    ''I know what it's like my friend. It's a hard life
with a twisted limb, but a splint will help it heal. Let's
see what I can do. Perhaps you will have better luck
than me,' I told him as I searched the area for some
suitable twigs.

    My grandmother had taught me many secrets of
the forest, and after collecting some healing plants I

rubbed their sap onto the injured limb before placing it between two sticks for support. With nothing to hold them in place I ripped the end of my shirt to make a bandage. A chill wind had blown up, but there were no small branches with which to make him a suitable bed. The only option was to break my walking cane into small pieces, even though it would make it harder to trek home without support. The cold bit into me as I laid my jacket over the makeshift nest, settled him in its warmth and began my journey home.

Several times I stumbled along the endless path as the rain soaked into my thin shirt. Exhausted and shaking I eventually reached my shack and tumbled thankfully into bed. My dreams that night were of the wounded animal, and I knew no matter what, the morning would see me retracing my steps to check on his welfare. For several days I struggled backwards and forwards across the countryside, but although my new friend's health improved mine worsened.

He was now almost totally recovered. I had done my duty and after one final visit I could rest. The path seemed never ending, my leg twinged and buckled with every step, and the stick I had found to replace my old staff offered little support. The animal emerged from his hiding place in the bushes as I drew near and came to stand by my side.

'You are healed now, my friend', I told him stroking his head. 'Free to return to your natural habitat so I will say goodbye and wish you Godspeed. Have a good life.'

He licked my hand as I turned to begin my final journey home, watching as I stumbled along the path. Twice I slipped on the rain sodden undergrowth sending pain jarring through my leg. Painfully struggling to my feet, I laboured along the trail until the village came in sight. Nearly home.

'Hey, twig boy. Where you been hiding yourself?'

It was one of my tormentors, standing blocking the path. His cronies emerged and surrounded me as I turned to try to escape.

'Leave me alone. Why are you picking on me? I've never done anything against you.' My voice came out in a tremble, and I knew this time I was in for a serious beating. In my weakened state I didn't stand a chance and could only appeal to their better nature.

'You're weird and I don't like you,' the fat one taunted as he kicked at my crippled leg. I fell to the ground, twisting my good limb as I put up my hands to cover my face.

'Let's get him.'

'We'll have a bonfire. Find some twigs. Oh, look we've already got some. Who's got some matches?'

They'd all been drinking. Were they serious? Who knew what they were capable of in that inebriated state? The numbness spread as they dragged me into the pasture, and I truly believed my time had come. A deep throaty growl cut through their maniacal laughter and they turned towards the source of the noise. Another snarl, a howl and four black shapes emerged from the shadows. Pandemonium ensued as the creatures attacked the gang, their screams cut through the still night air. Darkness descended.

I woke to find myself in my own bed. My leg felt wet with saliva, and eight eyes glowed at me in the darkness. Time had no meaning as I drifted in and out of consciousness until one day I woke from my coma feeling alive and hungry. Dawn was breaking but it was still dark as I became aware of gentle hands holding a beaker of water close to my lips.

'Good, you're awake,' a soft voice broke through my confused brain.

'Who are you? How did I get here?'

'Five days and night you have lain, Silvester, but when the fever broke we knew all would be well.'

'How do you know my name? It is many a year since I have been called anything but "Twig boy." You said "we." Who else has cared for me?'

'Look at your leg, Man of the woods. Nature repays those who care for her young. You gave the pup all you possessed, and in turn my companions cared for you. Stay strong.'

Was I dreaming? Four loud howls followed her words and then she was gone. Rising from my bed I knew something felt different; instead of being crippled my leg was straight and true. Like the trunk of a tree I stood robust and tall. No longer a twig boy, my act of random kindness had transformed me into a man of oak.

WHAT HAPPENED TO BUTTERCUP
Paula Harmon

'Well the thing is Mum, that …'

'You teenagers, you're all as flipping idle as each other…'

'No listen Mum, honestly, I did what you said…'

'No you flipping didn't. You couldn't wait to get back could you? You've probably got some mindless activity you want to do - like reading or summat. How're we supposed to manage when you won't pull your weight? If your father was alive to see you, he'd turn in his grave, he would. You couldn't even be bothered to go all the way to the Saturday market. It's not like it's far. It's not like it was hard. Ten miles it is. Five a.m. start I said. Be there by eight a.m. Stand there looking woebegone. Sell the cow. Come home with enough money to see us through the month. Lor' love a duck, it's not like it's brain surgery. Less blood for a start.'

'Yes but Mum, the thing is that…'

'Teenagers weren't like that in my day, oh no. You only had to look like you were going to answer back and you got the strap. That's where I went wrong with you, spoil the rod and spare the child that's what I did…. or summat like that. Anyway, when I was your age, I got the strap regular just for breathing, right across the posteriror. I did. Never did me no harm. I can sit on anything now. Can't feel a thing. Them princesses feeling peas through seven mattresses - wimps. I couldn't feel a boulder under one. That's if we could afford a mattress. Which we can't cos you didn't do the one flipping thing I asked you to.'

'Yes but Mum, I left at 5 a.m. like you said, and I started towards market but then there was this woman.'

'Haven't I warned you about them women? Haven't I? Look what happened to your Uncle Ethelbert. Thought he was having fun then his nose dropped off, then he started oozing and I'm not talking pores. That's what comes of them women. Now if you want a girl, Mabel's daughter's still up for grabs. OK so she's nearly forty and she ain't got many teeth, and none of her marbles, but she can bake a good loaf out of straw and it's not like she'll stray.'

'Yes but Mum, this woman was about an 'undred or at least your age and she said she wanted to trade for a cow.'

'Well if she wanted a cow, couldn't you have pointed her in the direction of Hildegarde.'

'Hildegarde hasn't got a cow.'

'Hildegarde IS a cow. Did you hear what she said about me last Wednesday?'

'Mum, you said you wanted me to sell the cow. I met someone who wanted to buy a cow. I sold her a cow. She paid for it.'

'She paid in beans. Beans. What the … fudge…. is the point of beans? An 'undred beans maybe - we could have boiled some and sold the rest on. But five?

Five beans? What the blue blazes can we do with five beans?'

    'She said they're magic beans. She said: 'plant them at midnight and tomorrow all your dreams will come true.'

    'That's MUSHROOMS lad. Magic mushrooms. Flip me. Teenagers these days. Can't even get their hallucinogens right. Best thing you get with dodgy beans is a runny bum. Next thing you'll be telling me is there's a giant with a golden goose that lays golden eggs living up a beanstalk. Sort your own supper out. I'm going to bed.

STRANGER BEASTS

VANDA
Val Portelli

Vanda was hungry, very hungry.

This wasn't surprising as she hadn't hunted for days, and even that had come close to being a disaster.

Normally, as long as she didn't laugh too openly and show her teeth she didn't have a problem, especially as her normal haunts were bars or clubs with dim lighting. Most men only noticed her beautiful figure and her 38DD breasts, which she displayed in low-cut tops, or her long, long legs which she showed to their best advantage in tiny mini-skirts, often paired with thigh-high boots. Despite her outfits she still managed to look classy but generally avoided the rich businessmen, as they were too likely to be remembered and missed more quickly.

Her last excursion had started off as usual. She had gone to a new disco that had already built up a reputation with the younger set, and she knew it would be crowded. There was no problem getting past the bouncers, they were too busy ogling her black leather outfit. Once inside she was able to use the crowd as cover while she picked out her victim.

She selected her target. The look on the poor guy's face would have made her laugh if it had been safe to open her mouth wide enough. When she made it obvious she was giving him the come-on, he kept looking around to see if she was actually directing her attention to someone standing behind him. Finally he got the message and plucked up courage to talk to her, or rather shout over the noise of the music.

With a mixture of lip reading and gestures she eventually got through to him the idea of going somewhere quieter. He rather shyly took her hand as they left the club together. She noticed the look on the faces of the bouncers as they went out, obviously bemused as to what a gorgeous girl like her was doing with a nerd like him. Damn. That meant they might remember her. Hopefully they would just assume she was out to earn some money, and the guy was a rich eccentric who wasn't able to get it any other way.

It was hard going but eventually she managed to persuade him she was a country girl at heart and enjoyed nothing more than a walk through the woods at midnight. Either that or he finally thought it was his Red-Letter day, and he was at last on a promise.

Although she had more strength in her little finger than most men had in their whole bodies, she was surprised by his power when he started stripping off her clothes. Propped up against a tree trunk she amused herself for a while as his passion grew, but then her hunger became too intense. Just as she was about to sink her teeth into the juicy throbbing vein in his neck he pulled away suddenly.

'Hey. Who's there?' he yelled. 'Show yourselves, you perverts.'

From a nearby clearing two of the bouncers from the club suddenly came into view, laughing hysterically. Through the red haze of her need to feed she was tempted to take on all three men. She knew she could beat them easily but the security guards would be too well known. They might even have told their colleagues what they were going to do, and her cover would be blown.

Frustrated she took off. Before they could come to their senses she was already a mile away. She managed to drain a few rabbits and other woodland creatures, but that was just an apéritif, nothing like the satisfying taste of a full eight pints of O positive.

Hence the reason she had to lie low for a few days and was now desperate for some sustenance. Dressing more demurely than her usual outfits, she put on black ski pants, a black T-shirt and threw a black leather jacket over her shoulder, before gliding down to a local neglected area.

It had been intended to be the site of a new block of flats. The old houses had been demolished but then the builders went bankrupt and the weeds took over. Now it was inhabited by tramps and drug addicts, with the occasional passing gypsies. The travellers would have been ideal but for the fact they always moved in large family groups. With their distrust of outsiders, it was too difficult to get one alone. Although the gentlemen of the road were a better target there was still a community of sorts, so the timing had to be right.

Vanda picked her way carefully over the rubble, moving closer to the small bonfires scattered around the area. It would have been quicker to glide but she didn't want to attract attention in case anyone was watching. She had got to know the area well and could even pick out the regulars. Her attention was drawn to someone sitting right on the outskirts, huddled around his own fire, as if he was not sure he would be welcome if he tried to move closer to the main groups. Perfect.

As an immortal she had all the time in the world, but she still found it hard to sit and watch her meal until, one by one, the fires died down and total darkness descended. After that it was easy. There was only a tiny yelp as she sank her teeth in and sucked until his wrinkled frame collapsed, but at least she had dined royally that night.

It was a myth that vampires were only nocturnal. Although she preferred the hours of darkness she had learnt how to deal with daylight. She still avoided the midday sun and preferred the overcast days, which was why she lived in England rather than her hotter homeland in Europe.

So it was that she was wandering through the woods on a typical autumn day; cold, windy and with a drizzly, depressing rain coming down. She had seen the "*No Entry*" signs but ignored them. After all, human restrictions didn't apply to her.

She heard a shout. 'Fast.'

Intrigued, she looked through the trees to see a group of people standing with bows in their hands and sets of arrows in quivers hanging from their waists. She had seen but ignored the other signs, *"Danger. Archery tournament in progress. All visitors please keep to the footpaths."*

All the archers had stopped loosing their arrows and were gazing in her direction. Perhaps they were worried about lawsuits if they injured someone. Vanda smiled to herself. There was no way a metal arrow could cause her injury or pierce her skin, even with a direct hit.

Suddenly her face changed.

She recognised the nerd from the night-club. He had a strange expression on his face. Perhaps he was pissed off at her for not bringing help when he was left alone to face the two bouncers.

Their eyes met as very deliberately he raised his bow, lined her up in his sights, and loosed his wooden arrow straight at her. In the seconds it took for the missile to reach her she realised this was a field shoot. They used wooden arrows, not metal ones.

Just before the wooden stake went straight through her heart she saw him as he really was, a werewolf, the timeless enemy of Vampires. It was her last conscious thought before she shrivelled into dust.

BAD HOUSEKEEPING
Paula Harmon

The spiders had been hiding in the loft for months. That little sac of eggs in the corner of the attic window which no-one could be bothered to dislodge in April had been forgotten. Such a tiny thing could surely only hold money spiders, perhaps it was a good omen.

In July, when the holiday suitcases were taken down, no-one noticed that the egg sac was distended, bloated. The lack of sunshine was put down to yet another disappointing British summer. Two weeks later, no-one even bothered to go into the attic to put the cases back, they were simply shoved over the edge of the hatch and the hatch was shut.

In September, the householders lay in bed and heard creaking from the attic.

'It's the beams contracting,' the spiders heard one of them say, 'the house is getting colder.'

'Are you sure it's not mice?' said the other human.

'If those are mice, they've got hobnailed boots on!' chortled the other, 'stop worrying, it's an old house.'

In October, the householders decided to go on a weekend break. The loft hatch was opened, the loft ladder pulled down with a screech.

How strange, there was no light coming from the attic, despite the window in the gable end and the fine Autumn sunshine outside.

The husband hesitated on the rungs but shrugging, clicked the external light switch and started up into the loft. As his head rose above the edge, four hundred enormous eyes surrounded him, four hundred hairy legs edged towards him, fifty mandibles clicked.

'AAAARGH!'

'Don't scream!'

'But it's hideous!'

A hundred hairy claws hooked into the human's jumper and drew him up into the attic.

'True…. but mother says they taste delicious. Tuck in. We're lucky he was too terrified to shout. With any luck, his mate will come and look for him soon and we can have a proper feast before finally getting out of this prison.'

VALENTINE'S DAY LOVE STORY
Val Portelli

She had a cold. Her nose was red from constant blowing, her stomach was bloated from the curse and her hair was in dire need of a wash and cut. It was a wet, miserable night, but having run out of coffee she had to make the late-night trip to the 24-hour supermarket. Perhaps while she was there she could pick up some medication.

Snuffling and shivering all she wanted to do was get home to bed. Browsing the medicine aisle she saw her preferred remedy, but typically it was on the top shelf and there was not an assistant in sight to fetch one down. Her balance was off-sync, so it was not surprising that as she stretched to grab the packet the whole display came crashing down around her.

With her face now as red as her nose she struggled to put them back into some semblance of order before anyone spotted her. Mortified at her clumsiness she became aware of the arm reaching to help before she registered the gorgeous male attached to it.

'Are you OK? You look a bit shaken up. Why don't you pay for your purchases while I finish putting these back, and then join me for a hot drink before you venture out again?'

She noticed the concern in his beautiful dark eyes, and although it wasn't her usual custom to respond to chat-ups by strange men, decided to accept his offer. Not only did he restore everything back to its proper place, he even carried her bags as she finished at the check-out. Gently taking her arm he led her into the cafe within the shopping complex.

The hot chocolate restored some colour to her ashen face as she felt its warmth seep into her bones. The heat of his gaze made her forget her sorry state, and as they sat and chatted she realised this was the man she had been looking for all her life.

Unbelievably, he seemed to feel the same way about her. It was love at first sight. He took her home, made her comfortable and visited frequently while she was recovering. When she was well again they dated regularly and she was full of anticipation when he booked a special meal for Valentine's Day.

Although she had only known him a few short weeks, she had no hesitation in saying "yes" when he got down on one knee and asked her to marry him. Despite only having a few friends as guests, her wedding was the happiest day of her life.

In their luxury honeymoon suite, she smiled as she remembered their first meeting. He was in the bathroom brushing his teeth as they prepared for their night of wedded bliss. Their romantic story would be something to tell their grandchildren in the years to come.

*****

The glow from the full moon reflected off the satin sheets as he slipped into bed next to her. Turning into his embrace she moved closer for their first passionate kiss as husband and wife.

That's when she noticed his extended canines and hairy body.

DEDICATION
Paula Harmon

Annie ran. Or rather, she tried to. Last night's blizzard had been a surprise. The roads were blocked, the paths were clogged, drifts lay six feet deep. But Annie wouldn't let a bit of snow stop her training. In the muffled, blinding dawn, she staggered on.

'You're stupid to go out in this,' murmured her husband before starting to snore again. Lazy, unsupportive pig.

Everyone said Annie was too out of shape. She ran early otherwise her children sniggered as they beheld her curves in unforgiving lycra, two support bras strapping down her chest, the curve of her stomach unhidden. Let them call her fat: she would be fit enough to raise money at the fun-run for endangered wildlife if it killed her. At least she was doing something.

The world was silent but for the whomp whomp of her plodding feet. The trail was usually full of runners, pacing along, earphones in, competing against themselves. But today Annie was alone.

The trail started in town but was soon in the wilds. On one side meadowland sloped down to the river and on the other, stony ground clumped up to a summit hidden in trees. Annie reached the stretch where everyone ran faster. An old building was hidden by a dark forest. There were high fences and warning signs. Even the town's older people couldn't quite remember what it had been in the war: house?

menagerie? research facility? lunatic asylum? The night runners and the early morning winter runners told of flashes of light, eyes perhaps, flickering behind the wire.

Annie was oblivious. Alone, with snow crunching under her slow feet, she hallucinated: imagining slipping back into the warm bed after thawing out under a hot shower. She couldn't have picked up pace even if she had remembered where she was. Her ankles stung, the cold air scratched her throat and dried her lips. Her heart protested with every thud thud of her throbbing feet.

Her eyes were closed, so she did not see that the fence around the forest had been brought down by snow. Creatures had emerged and stood on fallen warning signs, looking down on the trail, deserted but for one small, plump woman, red-faced, slogging along, her chest heaving.

In silent telepathy they fell into formation and streamed down the slope.

This one would be nice and juicy, once the lycra was chewed off.

Moments later, watching an inferior spit out the last support bra to expose the chest cavity, the alpha male reached in for the heart and liver.

Poor Annie, perhaps she should have listened to her husband this time.

It could be said that she'd always wanted to give her all for wild-life.

But probably she'd been thinking of something recognisable and maybe cute.

The pack, nourished, looked down the trail. The sun had risen. More fodder was approaching. Shoving Annie's remains into a ditch, licking the blood from the snow, they slinked into hiding and waited…

A DRAGON IS FOR LIFE
Val Portelli

It's that time of year when everyone has written their Christmas list and is waiting hopefully for Father Christmas to drop down their chimney. (Don't worry if you have central heating, Santa is an old hand at this and always finds a way to get to the mince pies.)

Drago wasn't sure he would get a visit. He had tried to be good all year, but sometimes he couldn't help letting out a heavy sigh, and when he did, he tended to set fire to things. Added to that his wings sometimes knocked objects over, and his tail was so long he couldn't always control it.

The OHDAR (Orphan's Home for Destitute Animals and Reptiles) had tried their best to find him a new home but without success. With all the children wanting pets for Christmas, the kittens and puppies had gone bounding out the door with their new owners, accompanied by expensive toys to make them feel at home. Once or twice visitors had shown interest in the dragon, but as soon as the staff explained how much attention he needed they always chose something easier, knowing the kids would soon get bored, and it would be down to the parents to take care of the new pet.

Add to that his long lifespan and it wasn't surprising nobody wanted him. It looked as if he would be spending yet another year in his small enclosure, alone, lonely and just wanting someone to love him.

There weren't any other dragons in captivity so he knew he would never meet a lady friend, and as an endangered species might even be the last of his line. Another deep sigh unwittingly escaped his lips, the fire alarm went off, and once again he was in trouble. Feeling miserable and with nothing better to do, he was sound asleep when he heard a clatter outside and looked up to see a jolly, fat man with a white beard.

'Ho, Ho, Ho and a Merry Christmas to you Drago. Have you been a good dragon this year?'

'I've tried to be, Santa, but things kept going wrong. Nobody wants me, and when I feel sad and breathe heavily things get burnt. I guess I'm on the naughty list this year.'

'Hm,' said Father Christmas. 'This is a difficult one. You're not really good, and you're not really bad. I've got an idea. Instead of having the flames cause problems how would you like to come and help me tonight? When we fly over the North Pole the tracks on the sleigh keep freezing up, and the reindeer say it makes it harder to pull. You could help to melt the ice and make it easier. What do you say?'

'I'd love to, but how do I get out of here?'

'No problem. I can sort that. Off we go then.'

At first the reindeer were a bit dubious when the dragon started flying alongside them, but every time they went over a particularly cold part of the world Santa gave Drago a wave, and he blew a gentle fire breath to thaw the frost.

He had a wonderful time, and although he was tired from all the flying he didn't want the night to end.

Finally, with all the presents delivered they returned to the North Pole for a welcome mince pie and a glass of Sherry.

'Well my lad, you did a wonderful job tonight and we got around in record time. You've definitely earned a place on the virtuous list. Now what present would you like?'

'The only thing I want Santa, is to live with a nice family all year round. I know so many animals at the shelter who find homes for Christmas, then are back soon after the New Year when the children get fed up with them.'

'I would never do that to you Drago. It's terrible when people treat living animals like throw away toys. You can come and live with me and Mrs Claus. With a few hot breaths now and then you can keep our fires going and help reduce the heating bills. After all, a Dragon is for life, not just for Christmas.'

And that boys and girls is why you don't see many dragons. They're all too busy helping Santa keep warm.

A PRIZE
Paula Harmon

And that autumn, my father, our chieftain, owing them tribute for keeping our hunters safe through the summer, invited the folk from the forest to a feast in our hill fort and we ate the lean fresh game hunted that day and we drank deep of mead and barley beer.

And then my father challenged their chief to a game and put up a prize of a box of fine pots and silver and jewels from the eastern traders, and their chief who was by far the better player, put as his prize, the hand of his dryad daughter to be my bride, safe in the knowledge that he could not lose.

And yet he lost.

And in Spring, he brought her to me as a bride and she was beautiful. Her skin was the silver of birch and her hair the brown of oak and her lips the red of berries and her eyes the green gold of beech and he placed her hand in mine and she looked at me.

But oh, when I saw her look out into the hills and meadows open to the sky, without refuge or sanctity of trees and I saw the lips quiver and the eyes fill, I could not take her as my bride. With a kiss to her lovely hand I bowed to her father and said that I could not take his sapling and plant it in the hills for I loved her too much to see her thrown and spun by storms and gales. And she kissed my cheek and smiled and her father smiled too and promised us safety from wolves through the winter and took her away.

Often, when I hunt, I wonder if she watches me from the undergrowth. I wonder if she could have loved me too one day.

But I am not sad, not really, for it is no prize if the prize did not wish to be won.

DRAGONS' REVENGE
Val Portelli

It had turned into one of those days. First I got up late, then rushing my breakfast I filled up with the wrong fuel which gave me indigestion all day. Trying to go about my business I became caught up in a fairy demonstration demanding equal rights. As usual the goblins had to get in on the act, so they started a counter demonstration blocking off all the airwaves.

The gremlins were supposed to be keeping order but in their normal way only succeeded in making things worse. I was caught in the middle of it and ended up with pepper spray on my wing which stung like hell, even through my thick skin.

When I finally reached the den for work my boss was in a bad mood and kept me late, so I hit the rush hour on the way home. Air works were causing the usual hold-ups, and the elves were too busy dancing and singing to organise the traffic.

When another dragon cut me up, clipping my wing and dislodging my mirror, I let rip and blasted him. Typically, it was a Viking Troll who came to take details. He insisted my identification should show both Runic and Latin translations following the latest directive from the International conference under Section 586, sub section three billion and two.

When I protested it had only been implemented a millisecond ago he insisted ignorance was no excuse, and it wasn't his fault the Witches had mucked up the distribution spell. He insisted on breathalysing me, and of course, with the fuel mishap this morning I came out over the limit.

'So that's the whole story your honour. By the way you might want to look at the labelling on your courthouse. To say the structure is "flame resistant" is misleading.'

PEN FRIENDS
Paula Harmon

It had seemed such a good idea. Daisy and Molly had been corresponding via social media for a year and having similar interests and being at a 'sensible' age, meeting up seemed like a nice risk-free plan.

Daisy knew that Molly was a 'sensible' age only from the content of her posts. Molly argued that she was not photogenic and hinted at some medical issue which made her shy of cameras; her profile pictures tended towards images of turquoise calligraphy surrounded by pink flowers. Admittedly Daisy's own profile picture had once been a cartoon hippo, but nowadays she displayed herself as she was: fine lines, wrinkles, grey hair and all.

Daisy had formulated a mental image of Molly as a glamorous woman, surrounded by antiques and fine china, writing romantic tales at midnight in turquoise ink and digitising them afterwards. Judging by the times of her posts and emails, Molly was a night owl, slumbering till late morning like a lady of leisure. She alluded to regular holidays in the Mediterranean and Daisy imagined her home would be luxurious and her IT equipment state of the art, despite the turquoise ink. Now and again Molly mentioned a shadowy man and while Daisy envisioned a butler or bodyguard, she sometimes wondered if his role was purely domestic. Molly wrote novels, which while apparently sweet, held an undercurrent of some hidden passion.

So all in all, when the opportunity finally arose when they could meet in person, Daisy was thrilled. She checked out the address Molly provided on 'streetview' and noticed that it was in a very leafy suburban avenue. So leafy in fact that it was hard to make anything out clearly, although it seemed rather grand. Molly's final email before the trip spoke of fine foods from her continental estate and Fetească Neagră from her own vineyard. Daisy looked up Fetească Neagră and salivated at the thought of blackcurrant richness. Reconsidering the £4.99 bottle of Pinot Grigio she had planned to take as a gift, Daisy splashed out on some Harrods chocolates instead. Then she went to a charity shop in an upmarket district for a designer outfit, so that she wouldn't look as impoverished as she actually was.

The day finally arrived. After a long journey by train, Daisy turned left at the station as Molly had directed and walked in the late afternoon autumn sunshine until she found the entrance to the avenue. Dusk was falling rapidly, darkened further by immense plane trees and tall walls. Were there several houses or was the wall for just one house?

Daisy hesitated, standing on the corner in her pre-loved Christian Dior and shifting the Harrods bag from hand to hand.

'You don't want to go down there, love,' said a passer by, making her jump, 'it's always a bit foggy and all them high walls and trees give me the creeps. Plus they're a bit posh for the likes of us.'

A little worried that perhaps she looked like second-hand Rose, Daisy remembered that she was a rational woman. It was darker and lonelier in her country hamlet with the nearest police station twenty miles away. She messaged Molly to say she was about to arrive and plunged into the avenue.

The house, seen through the enormous gates was certainly very impressive. Perhaps Daisy was surprised to see dragons on the gate posts instead of horses' heads or pineapples but she was more surprised to find the gates open before she'd even pressed the intercom, and to discover that crunching her way across the gravel drive took less time than it looked as if it ought to.

There was a fountain in the driveway but it wasn't running and the water, under late evening skies looked dark and viscous. Hearing the flick of a tail as she passed, Daisy would have peered into it, but a creak drew her attention to the heavy oak front door which was opening under a porch of ivy and virginia creeper. Beyond it she could see nothing but darkness, lit only with candles. Again, Daisy hesitated, but telling herself not to be silly, she mounted the steps.

A man awaited her, the butler presumably. As she had suspected he was young, very handsome and just looking into his dark lashed eyes made Daisy blush and her heart beat faster. Molly was a lucky, or clever, woman.

'Welcome,' he purred in velvet tones, taking my gift, 'her ladyship is just rousing from her… nap.

Perhaps you'd like to freshen up a little after your journey?'

In a small cloakroom, Daisy looked for a mirror and found none. Coming out into the empty hall, she found no mirror there either. She really wanted to check her appearance and feeling a little guilty, crept up the stairs to find a bathroom. The bathroom, opulent and ornate, also had no mirror and Daisy decided to sneak back downstairs and hope no-one had seen her. As she passed a bedroom, she heard voices low and throbbing:

A woman said 'what is she like, Gilbert?'

'Nice and plump but hardly in her first flush; though she's younger than you, by a century or three.'

'Don't be so cheeky!' the woman chuckled and Daisy heard a creak, not of springs but of hinges.

Peeping through the crack in the door, Daisy saw not a bed but an open wooden chest. At least... it looked like a chest.

As fast as she could, Daisy started to tiptoe along the landing, and then in desperation, slid down the banisters to avoid capture.

Catching her breath in the hall, she hobbled to the door and turned the handle … but it would not budge.

Behind her, languorous footsteps sounded on the stairs.

'Lovely to meet you at last!' called a soft voice.

At that moment, Daisy managed to open the door and stared out into the darkness.

How had night fallen so quickly? She looked towards the impossibly distant gates. Hadn't the dragons been facing the other way? Had their eyes been lit up before, flickering irregularly? Daisy heard a gloop in the pond under the fountain.

'Don't stand about getting a chill, there's snacking to do,' Molly said, grasping Daisy's arm.

Daisy turned to look into the face of a woman so pale, she was almost transparent. In the shadow of the door her lips were the colour of blackcurrants and her eyes were... turquoise.

Daisy kicked off her fake Jimmy Choos.

'Oh good, you're making yourself at home,' purred Molly but Daisy was legging it down the drive, the gravel cutting her fancy tights and soft feet.

As Molly watched Daisy trying to climb the gates despite the fact that she clearly hadn't been remotely nimble for at least two decades, she sighed.

'Rescue her before she breaks her neck, Gilbert,' she said, 'I thought she was dippy, but didn't think she was actually mad. We all need a stiff drink.'

'I told you to get the electrics fixed before she came, Grandma,' said Gilbert, 'and I really think you're too old for coloured contact lenses and goth make-up.'

'Maybe you're right,' conceded Molly, as Gilbert ambled down the drive. She noticed the glooping in the pond and frowned. Gilbert was right, the electrics needed to be fixed, it really wasn't wise to deprive water dragons of oxygen for too long. They could ruin everything.

GOING HOME
Val Portelli

The storm appeared from nowhere. One moment the elite of society were partying under the stars on the millionaire's yacht, the next they were diving below deck for shelter from the raging torrents. Designer gowns worth a fortune were ruined in seconds by the torrential rain, and spike heels became hazardous on the slippery surface.

It wasn't as if they were in tropical waters where sudden weather changes were expected; this was high summer in the middle of the Mediterranean. Normally the only major catastrophe would be running out of some exotic food before they could replenish supplies at the next port of call.

I was not one of the esteemed guests, just a lowly waitress who happened to be in the right place when a virus struck down the usual serving staff on the boat. The man in charge of the employees found me working in a dockside café, and in desperation had employed me on the spot. I jumped at the chance, assuming the clientele on the ship would be better than the drunken sailors where I was trying to earn a living.

Unfortunately, they were not a great improvement. Tetchy at having their idyllic lifestyle disrupted they took it out on the staff. The atmosphere became strained, and tempers frayed as the tempest continued throughout the night. Despite being such a modern vessel, the constant battering of the waves caused even hardy travellers to feel queasy, but I was one of the few unaffected. Surprisingly, although I had lived all my life in industrial towns, I had always felt at home on the sea.

There had been some confusion at my birth and I had never known my true parents. As I grew up my surrogate mother explained what little she knew of my background.

'We had never been blessed with children and by the time I reached middle-aged I had given up hope of ever having a baby of my own. Your father worked hard so we could afford holidays, and we took pleasure in visiting unusual places. One year, when we were cruising, the ship developed a problem and we were informed there would be a delay while they made necessary repairs. Rather than wait around on board we hired a small boat to take us to a nearby uninhabited island.'

'If it was uninhabited, how did I get there?' I asked.

'We were never really sure,' she replied. 'Your father was a keen amateur photographer and we spent a few happy hours enjoying the flora and fauna in a particularly remote part which appeared never to have visitors. He insisted we navigated across some rocks so he could take one final photograph. That's when we stumbled across a tiny beach hut. Time was getting on and we had just decided to return to the ship when we heard a weak cry for help.'

'Was that me?'

'No. You were only a few days old. When we went inside the first thing we saw was a fisherman, lying on the floor, surrounded by his catch. "Mer…Mer.." he gurgled, struggling to speak. That's when we heard you crying, and we discovered you, lying in a cot, covered in seaweed. There was no trace of your mother, but somehow we managed to take you both back to the ship. The doctor onboard tried his best but the man died, without ever uttering another word.'

If the fisherman was my biological father, it might explain why I had the sea in my blood. After all the formalities were completed they took me home with them, legally adopted me, and brought me up as their own. They called me Merissa, assuming he had been trying to tell them my name. Now they too were gone, and I was alone in the world.

On the yacht I was run off my feet trying to look after not only the guests, but many of the crew who were suffering from the effects of the raging storm. The next morning there was still no sign of the sun, and although the wind had eased, the rain continued to pour down from the heavens while the sea raged in protest.

By midday it was still as dark as night, as if the yacht had become marooned in a winter time warp. Suspicious whispers spread amongst the crew, and by late evening the Captain announced his intention of abandoning the trip and returning to dry land. There was still radio contact, and all other areas reported calm seas and glorious weather.

Later, I went up on deck for some fresh air, and to escape the constant demands of the passengers and the depressing atmosphere. Although it was only early afternoon it was pitch black when I heard voices a few yards away, although I could see no one.

'We have no choice now Captain. With radio contact lost we are at risk of being marooned. I've never known anything like this.'

'I agree. There is something weird about this situation. The sea might be cruel but she has always given signs for those who know how to read them. Even in winter the weather has never been like this here. You would think Poseidon is angry, and somehow we've been caught up in his argument. It's too risky to sail tonight but inform the crew to be ready at daybreak. According to our navigator we are only 50 miles from shore, so if nothing else we can replenish the stores and make a further decision once we've anchored.'

'Aye, aye, Captain. To be honest the crew will be pleased to escape this place. They've been nervy and unsettled ever since the storm hit. It doesn't feel natural and they're all a bit spooked.'

The two men returned below and I was left alone in the dark. The wind had eased slightly but the heavens were still releasing torrents of rain to crash into the stormy seas. The boat rocked and swayed as great waves caught it up, then pounded it back down into the turbulent water. I stayed on deck mesmerised, imagining I could hear the siren's song beneath the howling of the storm.

A blinding flash of sheet lightning illuminated the night sky, and in the distance I saw what appeared to be a small rocky island. Somehow I knew its craggy surface and hidden caves provided a haven for a myriad of sea creatures. A deafening crack of thunder and the boat rocked, throwing me against the railing and nearly tipping me into the raging sea. The vessel righted itself, but another crashing wave hit almost immediately and the yacht listed to one side. Water poured over the deck forcing it even closer to the waves, and in that moment, I knew it would capsize. Another flash of lightning revealed the gaping hole spreading along the side of the boat, and I knew the time had come. Taking a deep breath, I climbed the rail and jumped. Behind me I heard shouts and screams as the seriousness of the situation hit the passengers, and the staff tried to organise life boats.

Rather than hamper me, the waves pushed me in the direction of the island and I swam easily, breathing as naturally underwater as I did on land. Nearing the shore, I turned for one last look at the doomed boat. It was nearly submerged, but as the sun rose I saw people floundering in the water. For a moment I felt pity, but then I heard the siren's song and knew my mother was calling me home.

TREASURE
Paula Harmon

On a tropical island they captured a girl.

She was beautiful, skin and hair iridescent. She was locked up. The purer she stayed, the higher price she'd command.

From the hold the girl sang. Words unknown and yet understood: loneliness, bereavement, yearning.

Her song curled into the pirates' minds until they wasted away, tears mingling with the sea-spray. The ship drifted on, steered by music, until reaching land.

The harbourmaster unlocked the hold, finding nothing inside but a bejewelled bird.

It filled his ears with triumphant song. Then, still singing, it flew out and disappeared southward over the waves.

MERRY THE MERMAID
Val Portelli

Swimming around as usual Merry felt lonely. The dolphins had gone off to play elsewhere, and the swarms of mackerel had escaped to other waters.

Resting on an island at low tide, a tabby cat had realised the advantages of becoming her friend. Even though she had shared some of her fish he had suddenly run off and returned to dry land. Maybe he wanted to get home before the water cut off his escape route, or perhaps he had been frightened by the sight of the boat that had suddenly appeared out of nowhere, close to her underwater cave.

With nothing better to do Merry swam closer and observed the several humans on board. There were a couple of girls, lazing in their bikinis as if changing their skin colour to an unnatural shade of reddish brown could make them more attractive. Usually she avoided people as they were a strange race, only interested in voting for rulers to lead them, who they then disparaged for not delivering all the impossible things they promised.

It was a lot easier with only one sovereign, Poseidon. His word was law. You made sure you kept on his good side and he left you alone with none of this stupid politics, elections, and every animal trying to make a name for himself. Even the monster from the deep respected him.

Normally Merry would have swum quickly away to preserve the idea that mermaids were a fantasy, but for some reason she was drawn to stay close to the boat.

Maybe it was the tall, dark haired, blue eyed human she had spotted gazing out from the deck into the dark water. She imagined him diving into the sea and joining her in her underworld kingdom. There were plenty of legends to support the idea so it wouldn't be the first time.

Humans thought they knew everything but had no idea how the secret underwater world had developed. What they had discovered with their wet suits and underwater pods only touched the surface of the myriad of mysteries that had lain hidden from their sight for thousands of years.

She knew all about them from her Facebook page. They thought they were superior being able to contact friends all over their world. They had no inclination of the scope of the other environment beneath the waves, where the fish and amphibians were able to monitor their every move.

Obviously not every species could use social media, only the ones able to spend time out of water and exist in both environments. Even when she shared information about the strange habits of these land creatures with other aquatic species they wouldn't always listen. They looked on it as a source of amusement when they heard some of the human's far-fetched interpretations of the marine world.

The thing Merry found most difficult to understand was how humans related to their own kind. Emotions were not something the sea world really understood. They ate, they copulated, raised their young and then they died or were eaten by predators.

Pondering these concepts Merry knew she should swim away and hide from the humans. If they caught her she would be locked in a tank for people to gawp at and would never be able to escape back to her home in the depths of the open sea.

Despite her trepidation she found herself drawn to the boat and watching the man on the deck. She knew from the stories handed down to her by her Mother that mermaids were supposed to have the power to draw sailors down to their doom, but she had never actually put it to the test.

Lost in thought she was suddenly aware of eyes watching her. Looking up she found the handsome human staring straight at her. Without thinking she turned on her charm and observed as the man stood silently for a moment, still holding eye contact. Just as she dived under water to swim nearer for a better view she noticed he was waving to her.

As she resurfaced she heard a splash. With a flip of her tail and a twirl of her body she turned back in the direction of the boat. He had dived into the water and was signalling frantically as he swam towards her. Obviously her charms had worked, and he had been unable to resist her.

He was a strong swimmer, and she assumed he would be able to survive in the water long enough for her to lead him back to her cave, where he would find areas to breathe in the pockets of air. Whether he would be able to get back to the surface and his own world afterwards she neither knew nor cared.

This should be fun.

He was still waving as the distance between them shortened. Although she could swim twice as fast as him they would still meet at a safe distance from the boat. It wouldn't do to forget everything and find herself too exposed to the dangers from his companions, who didn't appear to have noticed he was missing from their craft.

She was smiling at the thought of the pleasure ahead, but he only looked scared and seemed to be shouting at her.

Perhaps he was excited at the thought of their unusual tryst but why was he not more cheerful? Why did he look so alarmed when they were now only yards from each other, and why was he was still gesturing with a look of horror on his face?

Following the direction of his gaze she glanced over her shoulder to see the jaws of the great white shark inches away from her. Damn. Instead of a night of lust she was going to end up as dinner.

Her last thought was perhaps there was something to be said for being ruled by weak-kneed politicians. She thought she had got away with being rude to her ruler yesterday, but obviously not.

Thanks Poseidon. Thanks a bunch.

HOW THE DRAGON GOT HIS FLAME
Paula Harmon

When the world was new: forming and reforming, heaving and twisting, spewing fire and splitting earth, the first men shivered under endless days of cloud and dust.

The wisest person guarded a captured flame. At night, they worshipped the flame which kept back the wild beasts and the bitter dark. In day, they worshipped the flame which dried their clothes and warmed their food.

But they were still cold. And wild beasts circled in the relentless night.

Only the dragon befriended them. They shared their hunting with him and he curved around the camp and the fire and the people leant against his soft hide. Purring, he told them about the worlds beyond their valley, their mountains. They begged him to carry them flying above the trees, above the cloud. They thought it would be warm, closer to the sun and they did not believe it when he told them of the coldness of the blue.

The dragon felt sorry for the people, shivering and huddling round their fire yearning for the sun. So he taught them to lighten the dark by treasuring friendship and laughter and song.

And he worked his magic. Flying above the forest, above the mountains, above the cloud, he hunted and captured rays of sunlight, carrying them in his mouth and thrusting them into the frigid rock and frosty streams until they froze into gold.

And he said, 'Come and look, people, here is a little of the sun for you to behold. It is cold but it will not rot or fade. It will sparkle in the waters and it will glint in the rock faces. It serves no purpose but for its beauty to make you feel warm.'

The people asked, 'What do want in return?'

The dragon replied, 'Nothing, my friends. Nothing but that you do not disturb the gold and that you share the knowledge of this magic without destruction. It is enough for you to know that it is beautiful, mostly hidden under your feet. If you seek to possess it, evil will befall you.'

But time passed and the people became numerous. They learnt not just to hoard flame but how to create it. They rarely called on the dragon as they sought mountain passes to other worlds. They learnt to make shelters and weapons. And as they multiplied, so they divided.

And soon it was not enough to have the strongest bow or the sharpest blade or the most beautiful features. Soon, a man's value was dependent on the number of things he possessed which he did not need. And the people looked for something which would shine and not rust or dim and they remembered the frozen sunlight and took flakes from the streams and fashioned them into jewellery for the most important people.

And the dragon was angry. 'Did I not warn you!' he cried, 'Did I not say that evil would befall you if you sought to possess this gift and keep it from each other?'

And the people said 'We're not afraid of you! You who live alone in the mountains and fly alone in the sky. Your hide is soft, your claws are small and you purr behind teeth like bone needles.'

And the dragon said, 'Feel my hide - it has grown hard with time and neglect! Look at my teeth - they have grown as large and sharp as flint daggers!'

And he slashed the gold from the chieftain's head and arms with a swipe of his wing and he reached forward with his scaly snout and swallowed the blazing fire around which they stood, and the camp became cold and the wild beasts came closer and for a while they huddled in silence, waiting for the dragon to die but he did not die.

The dragon's eyes grew red and narrowed. Then he opened his mouth and with the sound of volcanoes, of hurricanes, of thunder, he roared: 'Is it not enough to be warm and safe and happy? I was the one who captured the gold! If it is anyone's it is mine! And I will bury it deeper and I will guard it and from this day forward, we are enemies and I curse you with greed. Forever more you will dig and destroy and sift and fight and die for the sake of things you do not need; for things with no purpose or function except to be beautiful and forever more, you will measure your value by possessions yet will never have enough!'

The people cried, 'Give us back our fire!'

And the dragon roared again and flame came from his belly and he swung his head from side to side and burnt down the camp and the trees behind them, and swallowing the flame once more, he flexed his wings and flew back into the mountains.

And ever since, gold has been harder and more deadly to find and the dragon has been at enmity with man, the fire growing in his belly ready to destroy and overwhelm the greedy and the proud and the exploiter. And he lies in wait for the day when they dig too deep for treasures they do not need.

And he will consume them.

HOW THE UNICORN GOT HIS HORN
Val Portelli

Long, long ago the Unicorn was just an ordinary horse. 'Silver' however was a bit of a show-off and never stopped boasting to the others about his beautiful, unusual colour. He was also very nosy and forever poking into other people's business. As he was quite young the rest of the herd humoured him until eventually he got too big for his hooves.

The elders had a meeting and discussed what could be done.

'We could turn him black or white so he doesn't stand out,' one suggested.

'We don't want him looking the same as us,' some of the others responded.

'How about if we make his nose grow long like Pinocchio?' was another idea.

'That might stop him being able to eat properly. We don't want to be cruel.'

They decided to consult the wise old owl for his opinion.

'Cats have their whiskers, I have my sonar, and most animals have a means of knowing when they shouldn't go somewhere they are not supposed to,' the owl recommended. 'Why not put a bump on his head so every time he knocks it he's reminded he shouldn't be there?'

'That's a great idea,' replied the matriarch, and with a little help from the fairies a small lump appeared on Silver's head.

He still wouldn't learn but every time he started snooping and banged his head the swelling became a little larger. Often he would become stuck and have to twist and turn to get himself free. At first his long spiral horn only gave him something else to boast about, but as he grew older and learnt wisdom his uniqueness left him lonely.

The faeries took pity on him and when a young mare got uppity she received the same treatment. Although they had offspring they are still on the endangered species list, and that is why it's so difficult to see a baby Unicorn.

UNDERGROUND CAT
Paula Harmon

I am the underground cat.

I slink along the tube. My eyes, flashing in Stygian dark, startle drivers.

I seek comfort from travellers' ankles. In rush-hour, they barely notice; but at night they perceive flashes of topaz in the tunnel black, then feel sleekness spiral their legs and shiver.

I am not really here. I am as insubstantial as the suck and rush of air, the squeal and moan along the tracks.

Munching on ghostly rats, I've been lost down here a hundred years, looking for the way above the ground, where my spirit can finally dissolve into starlight.

THE RHUNICORN
Val Portelli

It wasn't fair. None of the others in the Unicorn park would play with me. I could run as fast as them and loved to play 'Horns' but they said I was too big and rough. Secretly I think they were jealous, just because they were 'uni-corns' and I was a 'bi-corn.'

OK maybe my skin wasn't quite as silvery grey as theirs, but it was still sort of grey. After all Mum was black and Dad was white so that made me grey.

I'm sure they were envious of my thick coat, even if it was a bit wrinkled. It was all well and good being sleek but I bet the midges and flies made their lives a misery. At least I could have a good wallow in a mud bath without worrying about looking unkempt.

One afternoon I overheard the two-legged animals saying they had finally found a new home for me. As they were helping me into the transport box I hoped my friends would at least come to say goodbye.

'Come on Rose, what are you waiting for? You must have been lonely here all on your own,' one of the handlers said. I'd forgotten the others were invisible to the two-legs.

After a short drive we arrived at the new place and I saw the sign above the entrance 'Welcome to Rynos Oruss Park.'

As I looked around I saw lots of others just like me. This was going to be much more fun than with the one-horns. No wonder humans didn't believe in Unicorns if they never showed themselves having fun.

TRAVEL RABBIT
Paula Harmon

Stanley abandoned sex, drugs and rock 'n' roll.

It was difficult. He was, after all, a rabbit. But he wanted monogamy and Mildred wouldn't stand for deviance. She moved on to Bob, Dave and Harry three minutes after rejecting him.

Devastated, he became a travel rabbit. You may think you've never heard of this ancient vocation but surely you've heard of the one who told someone she was late? You know, white fur, top hat, pocket-watch…

Now you're torn aren't you? Do you ask what a travel rabbit does or find out what a rabbit knows about drugs and rock 'n' roll?

Drugs is easy. Rabbits know more about hallucinogenic plants than a festival goer with a botany degree. That's why bunnies lollop within three inches of a stream of cars doing sixty. They're looking at the pretty fairies, man.

Rock n Roll? Rabbits have rhythm but not opposable thumbs: excellent drummers but really bad guitarists. And did you know that a certain very famous person based his moves on a rabbit called Elfin Perflee from Memphis,Tennessee?

Stanley was more of a balladeer than a rocker, but he considered ending his days in the lettuce patch which is the rabbit equivalent of drowning your sorrows. Only he didn't seek oblivion, he wanted love.

So travel rabbit it was. They go by public transport and they're invisible. The chap with the white fur and pocket-watch was breaking the first rule of the profession. (The girl he intercepted was actually travelling by omnibus when she fell down an unfilled pothole. This interesting fact was edited out of the final draft of the story.)

Travel rabbits are there to help by whispering things like 'you're late' or 'it'll be fine' or 'I'll wake you at Woking' and occasionally but not really often enough 'stop shouting into your mobile.' They've learnt to levitate at rush hour - it's that or be crushed.

After three months travelling the Waterloo to Exeter line, Stanley forgot Mildred. He needed all his strength to support the lonely, nervous, weary, disappointed and bankrupt.

One busy night, Stanley hovered, millimetres from the ceiling, barely able to breathe. When the doors opened at Basingstoke, people swarmed on. Swept in was another travel rabbit, squashed between travellers, slipping towards certain death. Stanley, breaking the second law of travel rabbits, stood on a commuter's head and pulled her up just in time. He levitated her into the luggage rack where her slight frame trembled, her fur tousled, her eyes big with terror. He smoothed her ears and breathed words of comfort.

Station by station the train emptied. Stanley didn't notice. He was holding the most beautiful bunny in the world.

'I'm Peronelle,' she whispered.

'Marry me,' Stanley mumbled, his heart thudding in his ears.

There was not even a pause.

'Just me?' murmured Peronnelle, 'Oh yes! At last, I've found my soulmate. Of course I will!'

And they knew not why, but the last few weary passengers, rocking with the train on the last leg of their long journey, heard whispers of love and their hearts warmed.

STRANGER EVENTS

FINGERS
Paula Harmon

'Let me in.'

A hoarse gasp filtered through the filthy window. Someone's palm pressed desperately against it.

I slid along slimy walls to avoid the blood on the floor and the advancing hand. Just a hand, creeping towards me, its nails scratching on the floor.

As I made it to the glass, the voice came again.

'Let me in.'

I rose to open the window and saw…not a person but just an arm, and behind it more detached hands gathering, all pointing at me. And as I paused, I felt long rough fingers wrapping themselves around my ankle…

NEEDLECRAFT
Paula Harmon

Colours twisted in chaos until order emerged.
Whispering love, she knitted a uniquely patterned
sweater. Kissing the white cotton every time she
threaded her needle, she embroidered his undershirt;
near invisible soaring birds and full-sailed ships to
bring him swiftly home.

    If only he had been faithful.

    After she heard, her scissors ripped the sails and
broke the wings. She crocheted a scarf to cross over his
treacherous heart, her hook slippery with drowning
tears.

    When next he came back to her, she only
recognised his waterlogged body from the patterns she
had woven into his sodden clothes.

HOUSE SHARING
Val Portelli

'This house is freezing.'

'It's not really that bad Jack; it's just been empty a long while. Now we're here let's at least look round. Will you please stop playing with your phone and show a bit of interest. Emma, what do you think?'

'It's alright I guess. At least it's big enough to have my friends stay over. You'll have to pick them all up though; it's miles from anywhere. Unless I had a car, of course.'

Teenagers! They would be the death of me. Since Colin left to go off with his flighty-piece I'd had enough to put up with, fighting his solicitors to get enough to buy a home for the three of us, juggling work, finances, house-hunting and finding an area where we could afford to live.

Even before that I had the stress of trying to keep the peace while the kids took their exams. Things hadn't been going well for quite a while, and I didn't want the atmosphere between Colin and me to affect their future. He had promised the twins a car each if they did well, but now it was down to me to fulfil his promise. It wasn't as if he couldn't afford it, but that young, skinny bitch was out for all she could get and was determined to make him forget all his responsibilities to his family.

This house had looked good from the estate agent's description, five bedrooms, two ensuites, plus a separate family bathroom, a three-car garage and even a swimming pool. Most importantly it was within my budget, and as I walked round I could see why. The pool was a slimy green insects' delight, half filled with rubble. The property looked as if it hadn't been lived in for years, and every room would need major updating before I even thought of decorating.

It would need total rewiring and I'd have to install Wi-Fi if I wanted any peace at all. Somehow I would have to persuade Colin to cough up some more maintenance to cover the costs or we would end up on the streets.

*****

'Mum, what are all these people doing in our house? Can I bother them?'

'No, Amelia. I've told you before. We don't mix with their sort.'

'But they've thrown away all my things, and they're even clearing out where I drowned. There's no peace any more. Everywhere I go there's something in the way.'

'I know darling. I'm finding all these waves a nuisance too. I'll have a word with great Grandpa and see what he suggests.'

Everyone gathered for the family conference, five generations, and enough for a witches' coven with all of us together. We agreed the taking-over of our space had to stop, but there was a dispute about how it should be achieved. The older ones favoured the traditional moving of objects, noises in the night and opening doors and cupboards. The younger ones wanted to try more modern methods involving ectoplasm and actual physical contact.

Naturally great Grandfather had the final say and we were all given our haunting duties for a month to see if we could drive them away. Meanwhile we covered our ears to the constant barrage of sound waves emanating from all their gadgets and tried to avoid tripping over the beams.

*****

'Mum, tell her. She's moved my phone again.'

'I haven't touched your rotten phone. And don't go in my room messing up all my stuff or you'll be sorry.'

'I haven't been in your room, and I wouldn't touch your smelly stuff with a bargepole. It's you who's been rummaging through my wardrobe and leaving the door open. I'm going to put a lock on it in future.'

'For goodness sake. Haven't I got enough on my plate without you two constantly bickering. It might help if you cleared up a bit after yourselves instead of leaving everything to me. I'm forever putting the open packets back in the larder when you've finished with them. It's not a lot to ask.'

It was all getting too much. I had to leave the room before I burst into tears or started screaming. Actually, I was a bit bemused myself. They were good kids really, and although they were typical untidy teenagers their phones and iPads were not usually more than an inch away from their ears.

There was also the mystery of the dried fruit packets being split open and left strewn around the kitchen. Neither of them liked it and I had forgotten it was there, left over from Christmas. Maybe there were rats or something; another thing to add to my never-ending list of things to sort out.

I know there are noises in any old house and creaking floorboards are just the warped wood settling down, but since the renovations had been completed they seem to have got worse, not better. Perhaps it was time to cut my losses and find a small flat somewhere closer to town. It would be cramped, but the kids would be moving on in a few years, and this house was too big to wander around in on my own. It was too remote for my original idea of running a small guest house, even if it was quite a lovely home now it had been updated, and I would miss my early morning swim.

*****

'Colly-poos. There's no way I'm staying in this God-forsaken place. It gives me the creeps. There must be a decent 5-star hotel even out here.'

'It's only for one night sweetie. As the next of kin, I need to be here to sort out my wife's estate.'

'How odd that all three of them drowned. I often thought she was a bit unhinged, and living out here must have been the final straw.'

'Cornelia, that's a terrible thing to say. You know the coroner ruled it was death by misadventure. Actually, this is quite a beautiful place. I could easily turn it into the computer hub for my businesses. I wonder how strong the signals are out here.'

Listening to the conversation all sixteen of us decided we needed to take action tonight. I had a feeling the Mum of the newcomers would take great delight in scaring the designer panties off Cornelia. Revenge is sweet, especially when you're a ghost.

AN EMPTY VESSEL
Paula Harmon

I wanted a gift to remind my friend, landlocked in
Switzerland, of the sea she missed so much; something
unique but small enough to take in hand luggage.
Arriving late at a remote craft shop when it was about
to shut, I found a sculpture like a wave, curved and
irregular; iridescent blue edged with a froth of white. I
thought it was a small vase but it was filled in just
below the edge.

The vendor came over and said 'I'm fond of that
even though it's not quite right.'

He paused. 'Business was bad. I'd come in to
find things smashed, clay dried out, once even a dead
cat. The day this pot sealed itself up in the kiln, things
started turning around. So I think of it as a lucky piece.'

Good bit of spiel I thought. *It will entertain my
friend.* I pulled a dubious face, he knocked off a few
quid and I took it home to put in my suitcase.

*****

The flight was not busy, but I stowed my bag
carefully overhead. I sat in my aisle seat, wincing when
an inebriated passenger squashed his case next to mine
and then, tripping over my legs, fell into the window
seat and started to peruse the drinks menu. Cabin crew
followed, subduing bags and forcing the bulging
lockers shut. Halfway through the journey, everything
started to shake. I could hear luggage shifting above me

and when the plane lurched, all the lockers popped open.

As quickly as it had started, the turbulence ceased. A crew member came to reorganise things, sooth nerves, and remind the person between me and the drunk that his seat-belt should be on...the person who hadn't been there before. We looked at each other.

'Thank you,' he said, his voice musical. His aftershave was richly spicy and his clothes were made of a clinging silk which didn't look suitable for a Swiss November. His eyes had the depth of universes. I blinked.

'I am in your service,' he intoned.

'Who're you?' slurred the drunk, 'Where you from?'

'I'm a djinn.'

'I'm a bourbon if you're buying,' sniggered the inebriate.

The djinn repeated, 'I am in your service. I will grant you up to three wishes, for I was cruelly imprisoned and you have released me.'

'I wish you had warmer clothes on,' I said before I could stop myself and boggled as the silks were replaced by tweeds. The drunk stared and turned to the coffee options on the menu.

'I will stay with you, master, and watch over you every day,' said the djinn.

'Honestly you don't need to bother.'

I definitely need this break, I thought.

'But master, two more wishes…'

'I wish you'd leave me alone,' I said, closing my eyes and putting my earphones in to block him out.

*****

I lost him in customs then forgot him entirely. As ever, my heart leapt when I saw my friend waiting for me, achingly lovely. I dug about in my bag for the gift and found that it had a hairline crack and the lid was detached.

'Never mind,' she said, 'it's beautiful anyway.'

She flung her arms around me and I mouthed my longing into her hair.

With a soft chime and the scent of cinnamon, shimmering lights appeared then faded.

My friend looked up. 'I didn't realise it until now, but I've always loved you. Could you love me?' she said.

Out of the corner of my eye, a man in tweeds with a shimmering silk cravat and eyes like universes, raised a hand, smiled and disappeared.

HALLOWE'EN CONVERSATION
Val Portelli

'Why are all these people wandering around in silly costumes and masks?'

'It's called Hallowe'en. Sometimes it's called All Hallows eve, the day before the 1st of November when people traditionally honoured their dear departed.'

'But what's that got to do with the pumpkins and the scary stories, and children saying Trick or Treat?'

'It's the night when ghouls and souls arise from the dead and return to mingle with those still living. Perhaps they want to remind their loved ones about visiting their graves to lay some flowers and clean them up a bit. You know how mucky the stones can get if nobody takes care of them. Trick or treat is a bit commercialised now, but originally it was thought the witches would challenge people to try and trick them, or give them a treat if they gave the right answer to their riddles. Mind you, I've never known a witch who kept to the bargain. All they were after were puppy dog's tails, or newts for their cauldrons.'

'Are all witches bad then? What about the white ones?'

'Personally, I don't think they should be called witches. You don't see them flying around on broomsticks and annoying people. All they do is use herbs and nature to try to heal.'

'I wouldn't mind some of those sweets though. Do you think if I drifted over they might give me some?'

'That wouldn't be a good idea. I know you're young, so you've never had a chance to understand the way the world has changed. In the old days there was a lot of superstition but on the whole people were dutiful, and didn't need reminding to look after their dead. It was a sign of respect and the accepted thing to do. They didn't need all this advertising and marketing which is really just a way of making money.'

'It's not fair. Why can't I have some sweets?'

'You know you can't eat them, son. Don't let them corrupt you. Now we'd better get away from these crowds before someone sees us.'

'Would it matter if they did?'

'It's best not to put it to the test. Despite all their laughing and joking it would really scare them to know we exist. They're just pretending but seeing real ghosts could affect their minds. We've had our night out. Best we get back to our graves ready for our visitors tomorrow. Come on lad, that warm soft earth is waiting for us.

THRESHOLD
Paula Harmon

On the cliff, the girl spun.

The sheep behind her bleated and turned their backs. Below her, the sea was mesmerisingly far and heavenly blue.

Can you look down into heaven? she thought, *Is that what's calling me?*

She turned again to catch the voice. If the sea was not calling, then was it a shepherd? But the sheep were masterless.

Beyond the fields was the indifferent road. Cars flashed east to west, west to east, ignorant of all but direction.

'This way, this way.'

The voice bounced from ridges to terraces, ancient and nameless on the windswept land.

The girl took another step to the cliff-edge. Flakes of orange earth crumbled under her toes, disappearing into the space where the seagulls whirled above the waves in their intricate aerial ballet and down onto the distant shingle.

Would it hurt to fall? she wondered.

Would the seagulls part or would their beaks and feet slash as she dived? Would the air sting as it rushed past her face? Would the sea be at last, a pillow to engulf her? Or would she, as delicate as a fern or shell, smash into a thousand fragments yet become imprinted on the rocks, encapsulated forever.

'This way, this way.'

It was not the sea calling her to its turbulent heaven. It was the peaceful land.

Falling to her knees, she crawled back from the edge, the wind whipping her tear-drowned hair.

'Not yet,' she heard, 'turn this way. Try once more.'

DREAM WORLD
Val Portelli

For several weeks I hadn't been sleeping properly, and it was affecting my work. I felt lethargic all the time, and it was an effort to force myself out of bed to face the day ahead. A visit to the doctor became the obvious answer.

'How long has it been like this? Are you under any particular stress? Money worries? Boyfriend problems?'

'No, not really, well sort of. He has been a bit off lately, and I was annoyed when he used my credit card, but that's being sorted out.'

'Do you live together?'

'No, he lives up north so only comes down for long weekends, but I was thinking of finishing with him anyway. I can afford to lose the money, it was the sneaky way he did it which upset me more.'

'I'll write you a prescription for some sleeping tablets, but only for a week. They're fairly new, and getting addicted won't solve the underlying problem. No watching gory films or reading exciting books before bedtime. Hot chocolate, and a warm bath should help, but don't take them earlier than 20 minutes before you intend to sleep as they could make you drowsy and disoriented. If you're not better in a week come back and see me again, and we'll try something else.'

'OK. Thank you, Doctor.'

It was Thursday so I decided to take the first one the following night; that way it wouldn't matter if I overslept on Saturday. On the way home I picked up a slushy romantic novel, and some exotic oils for pampering in the bath on Friday night.

Something woke me from where I had been snoozing under a large oak tree, in the middle of a meadow with the warm sun beating on my face.

'Is she dead? Poke her again.'

'Oy. That hurt.'

'What are you doing in our field? This is private property.'

The voice came from one of the three people surrounding me, who bore a startling resemblance to garden gnomes. The one who had spoken even carried a fishing rod, and the one next to him looked as if he was made of concrete, and had a large chunk missing from his shoulder. 'Fish and chips,' I thought, then burst out laughing when I noticed the third one was wearing a jacket with the letter 'P' prominently displayed on both the front and the back. Fish and chips and peas!

'Don't lay there giggling. Get up. There's work to be done,' Fish said, as he struggled to pull me up. In the distance I could see a gingerbread house, and dutifully followed them as they headed towards it. Although I was only 5'5' I had to bend down to enter through the low door. Inside, the diminutive furniture resembled a large Wendy house.

'Sit down. Dinner's ready,' I was told as I tried to squeeze myself into one of the small chairs set round a miniature table. Delicious smells made me realise I was hungry, so I didn't immediately notice who had put the bowl of soup in front of me. Something caught my eye, and I realised tiny fluorescent fairies were working in pairs to carry the pots and serve the gnomes. The first course was followed by a laden plate with a full roast dinner, and there was even a tiny portion of blackberry pie and ice cream for dessert.

'You'll have to come and help if you intend to stay the night,' Chips informed me when we had finished eating. It was quite difficult to follow him up the stairs, as my feet were too big for the treads. In the cosy bedroom I could tell my feet would hang over the end of the bed.

'Make yourself useful. Pull that chair over and put it at the end otherwise a giant like you won't fit,' he told me. Somehow, the sleeping pills were in my pocket, and I took the second one before the best night's sleep I'd ever had. During the following days I used my height and strength to help the gnomes in their daily chores, and time sped by. It was only when I took the last tablet from the packet that I realised I had already been a week in their company.

'I'll have to go home tomorrow,' I told my new friends. 'Thank you for having me.'

'Not sure about that,' Peas replied. 'No one has ever gone away before.'

A strident ringing woke me the following morning, and I opened my eyes to see the alarm clock on my own bedside table. What a peculiar dream, but the rest had done me good. I felt full of energy and determined to give the whole house a proper spring clean over the weekend. The answerphone was flashing, and the numerous messages confused me.

'Tania. Are you OK? You didn't turn up for work and we were worried you might be sick.'

'Tania. It's Mum. Just checking it's still on for next week's meal for your Dad's birthday. Give me a call to confirm if Steve's coming down.'

'Hello. It's normal courtesy to phone in if you're sick. Please let me know when you're coming back to work.'

For a moment I was bewildered. I'd taken the tablet on Friday night, so today must be Saturday. Then why was the empty packet lying on the table? My phone told me it was the 15th. That was ridiculous; it would mean I had lost a week. Opening the front door, the first thing I noticed was three garden gnomes on the small patch of grass on the front lawn, which apart from the dustbin and a few weeds was normally empty.

The letterbox was overflowing, and the week's newspapers were piled high on the step, including the Sunday edition with its additional magazines. Picking them up I spread them over the kitchen table and found the latest one. It was the 15th. I must have slept the whole week, and if it was Friday I should be at work. If I rushed I might just make it, although I had no idea how I would explain my absence on the previous days. Perhaps I could say I had flu and was too ill to get to the phone.

'Do you want your toast well done?'

The voice startled me. I turned to see the slice of bread slowly turning golden brown as the dragon breathed on it. Whatever was in those pills, I'd happily take them for the rest of my life, as long as the housework fairies accompanied them.

TICKET DUDE
Paula Harmon

Wedged into the seat at the back of the carriage with my case and bag, I've balanced my laptop and started to write. Even on the way home there's no rest from work but at least no-one can read over my shoulder here.

'Tickets please!'

Ten minutes into my journey I proffer my ticket with one hand, trying to stop the laptop slipping with the other.

'That's fine,' says the collector, handing the ticket back having scribbled his approval.

An hour later:

'Tickets please!'

This time, my laptop nearly slides to the floor as I open my purse.

Scribble scribble, ticket handed back.

Half an hour on:

'Tickets please!'

Sighing, I take my time. Let him wait.

As I rummage, he says, 'where to?'

'Westbury, we're nearly there,' I snap, bending my fingernails on the recalcitrant ticket and handing it over.

'Westbury is what's on the ticket. Where would you rather it said?'

I close down my laptop with its drowning emails and impossible targets and look at him in surprise. The sunshine through the window is glinting on his poised pen.

'The Bahamas would be nice,' I joke.

As I bend to get my things together, he scribbles something on my ticket and hands it back, moving on, just as the train pulls into Westbury.

Only as I get out of my seat and look out of the window, the White Horse is missing. In fact the hill is missing, and so is the landlocked town. Instead, the platform is on the edge of a beach and there is a table on the sand under a sunshade. I can just make out my name on a reserved label.

Astounded I get off the train and find someone is waiting to hand me a cool drink and a sunhat. Behind me the train moves on, my briefcase and work laptop still on board. I stand there in the blazing sun with nothing but an overnight bag, a credit card and the words on my ticket obliterated but for the words:

'Bahamas - needs never return unless she wants to.'

THE AUTHOR'S TALE
Val Portelli

Thud! There it was again, the same noise I'd heard earlier in the day which I'd assumed was the workmen renovating the derelict cottage next door. The chiming of the clock made me jump. Midnight, the witching hour.

Perhaps I shouldn't have worked so late but the story was flowing, and after suffering the infamous writer's block for the past week the words had finally started pouring out of me. You know the feeling; you blame anything and everything when your publisher is pushing but your brain just won't function.

'Christine, maybe you should get away for a while. Stay somewhere peaceful. How about Scotland? It's beautiful at this time of the year, and if the weather turns it would be a good excuse to stay indoors and do some writing.'

Although it sounded friendly I could sense the underlying threat if I didn't meet my deadline. I'd have to cross that bridge when I came to it. The cottage was quaint but fully equipped, one of a pair, and when the taxi driver dropped me off it didn't seem that far from civilisation. It was only as night fell I realised the darkness of the highlands was not the same as the darkness of suburban London. At least there was internet and a surprisingly good signal for my mobile when I phoned to update my publisher.

'Hi Chris. Everything OK?'

'Brilliant. I can't believe this air. I walked for miles today. The problem is I'm eating like a horse, everything tastes so much better.'

'What about the book?'

'As usual you were right. I needed to escape to get my Mojo back, but you might have to consider revising the marketing. I know I made my name through romantic novels but this is different. Believe me; it's going to be a blockbuster. You'll have the first draft in a week or two but it's going to be the best thing I've ever written. Now leave me in peace, the words are calling me. Catch up when you've read it. Bye for now, and thanks. This was exactly what I needed.'

I had been in storms before, but nothing like the one that hit that night. The power went off, the thunder showed its anger, and the lightning displayed its contempt for electricity by illuminating the landscape to the village and beyond.

Waking from a restless sleep the following morning I braved the rain to investigate the adjoining cottage. Maybe I just needed the comfort of human contact. The door was opened by a guy in a checked shirt, bibbed baggy overalls and a high, odd shaped peaked cap. He seemed friendly enough but his accent was so broad I could only understand one word in four. I gathered the cottage had once been owned by a novelist who wrote ghost stories, and the workman didn't seem at all surprised when I explained the reason for my being there.

'Och Aye. Alice always did love her literary folk. Just don't take her way out lassie. We'll be gone soon and it can get lonely up on these moors.'

The rain had stopped when I went back to my temporary home. I headed straight for my computer with the words demanding to be set down. Although there was still no internet connection, power had been restored and my hands flew over the keyboard. The thud and striking of the clock made me realise I had been sitting at the computer for fifteen hours without a break. That day set the tone for the following weeks. The voice in my ear demanded I carry on until my eyes were blurred and my fingers bleeding, but she would not let me rest.

Occasionally I rebelled and shouted at the empty air 'I write romance. This is not my story.'

As I typed the final words 'The End' I heard Alice's voice for the last time.

'You have done well. Finally, my story is told. Now we can rest.'

*****

<u>Publishers Note:</u>
The author Christine Fairfax was well known as a successful romantic novelist. Her final work 'The author's tale,' was written under the pen name of Alice McSheeley. Despite being a change of genre, it remains the year's number one best seller.

The launch date for the publication of her book on the 31st October 2017 coincided with her untimely death, alone in a remote cottage. In accordance with instructions found near her completed manuscript, royalties from the sale of her books were used for the development of an annual writer's competition 'The McSheely opportunity.'

The prize is slightly unusual in that it includes a compulsory month's stay in a Scottish cottage owned by her estate. The solitary confinement is to allow fledgling authors the opportunity to finalise their own book without the distraction of outside influences.

The 2018 winner told us 'I've already packed and can't wait to spend a month in the cottage. It's a wonderful opportunity to have the solitude to finish my own novel which I know will be a best-seller. I'm eternally grateful to the late Christine Fairfax for the chance to follow in her footsteps.'

SOFT SOAP
Paula Harmon

'Milkmaids have it all their own way,' thought Marigold, plunging her sore, reddened hands back into the lye and pummelling the filth from the clothes. Her eyes filled but she shook her head in irritation at her own weakness. Tendrils of damp, bedraggled hair fell over her shiny pasty pock-marked face as she leant over the steam. 'Who'd look at the village laundress?' she asked herself pointlessly. The answer was obvious: no-one. Except Giles once, when it was dark and he was drunk and there was nobody to help her.

Marigold heaved the clean washing into a basket so she could put it through the mangle outside. She visualised herself winding the handle, the muscles on her blotchy arms bulging through her damp sleeves, the messy hair, the indoors face, the soap and splashed dirt on her skirts. Meanwhile, over yonder, Tansy was simpering over a fence, swinging her empty buckets as she talked to Giles. Not talking; whispering. He was having to get closer and closer to listen. Tansy was giggling and casting her eyes down. Everyone knows that milkmaids never get smallpox and her perfect skin was gently flushed with maidenly blushes. Her lovely hair was neat under her bonnet, which Giles was just now pushing back so he could put a rose bud over her ear.

Pausing to stretch and nurse her sore back, Marigold felt a brief tinge of guilt. Perhaps she shouldn't have gone to Granny Wormwood for that potion. Looking into the basket, she felt certain that a slight glow was coming from the laundry she'd washed.

Tansy wandered over, swaying her hips. 'Hope you've washed my best petticoats properly Mangold?' she said sharply, no longer whispering but using her normal voice and the childhood nickname.

'Oh yes,' said Marigold calmly. 'I did a special whites load just for your petticoats and stockings and oh, look, also Giles's undershirt and stockings. It seems like they're in a right pickle.'

Tansy sniggered, 'Oh fancy! My petticoats and his undershirt all tangled up together! Could be an omen! If I play my cards right, we'll be tied together pretty soon.'

'Reckon you're right,' said Marigold. 'And you'll be tied together just like these garments are. Only you won't be able to separate like these will and the stains will grow and nothing will take them out.'

'Oh Mangold, you do go on,' snapped Tansy, 'You always were a dilly daydream and no-one ever knew what you were talking about. Just hurry up and get those things dry. I want to be ready this evening to meet Giles in the lane where it's all dark. I just know it won't take much to get him to make love to me and then…'

'And a month or so later, when he raises that veil, you'll see each other exactly as you are. Exactly as you are. Dirt and all,' whispered Marigold.

But Tansy walked off without listening.
In the sun, the washing shimmered.

THE GRAVEYARD
Val Portelli

Nobody ever came to this old part of the cemetery. Even at Christmas, when relatives laid floral wreaths on the newer graves to show how dutiful they were, these memorials lay unloved and untouched. Some dated back to 1800 so perhaps there was no one left to mourn, even if the wording could have been deciphered to identify the correct one.

That's why I was surprised to hear the crunch of footsteps on this dark and bitter night, as a shadowy figure walked along the once regular aisles. Time and nature had taken their toll, and I watched as a figure criss-crossed between them, occasionally stopping and using gloved hands to wipe away the hard-packed snow on the tombstones.

I sank back into the shadows as he or she, I couldn't tell which, bent to read the wording, then stood sighing before moving on to the next one on their list. Who were they looking for? I knew every tomb in this area, and could have directed the visitor, but that was not the way things were done.

Finally, the man came close to the fallen cross, and spent time carefully examining the wording, as he compared the grave with a photo in his hand. Seeing how much his features resembled mine was like seeing a ghost, which was quite ironic in the circumstances.

'I've found you at last Granddad. It will take time but I'll make it up to you. In the new year I'll get a stonemason to repair the cross and visit you every week until things are put to rights. The true story will be told, you can depend on me, even if the rest of the family maligned you.'

I watched as he walked away but knew he would keep his promise. Finally, I would be able to R.I.P.

SOMEWHERE ELSE
Paula Harmon

Jo climbed the tree fast.

'Hang on,' I said, pulling myself up after her.

The branches shuddered. Old twigs shook loose and caught in my hair.

'They won't see us up here,' I argued, 'Not in all these leaves.'

Jo paused. Her face was rippling with green light as the swaying slowed. It was hot.

'Did you know,' she said, 'when you get to the top of something, right to the top, the top of the tallest something, then you can reach Somewhere Else.'

She was always saying this sort of thing, with utter certainty, dragging me in.

I made a tiny gap in the leaves. Were the boys and their snarling, slavering dog still hunting us?

'This isn't the tallest tree in the woods,' I pointed out. Further up the ridge were larches, looming and angry even in summer.

'It's the tallest tree in this bit of the woods.'

'Well I've been up the top of Bryn Cawr and didn't find Somewhere Else. There was just rock and dirt and a dead sheep.'

Jo twisted on her branch and looked over to the mountain across the valley. It looked like a fat, lumpy sleeping giant.

'Mountains ought to be pointy,' she argued, 'and anyway, Bryn Cawr isn't the tallest mountain around here.'

'Shh,' I hissed. The bracken was moving; the boys were crouched down, sneaking. Did they know where we were?

Jo shinned up the tallest branch. There were bloody scratches on her soft legs. I looked down, it was a long way to fall.

'Come back,' I begged.

'No. I want to be Somewhere Else.'

If she fell, she'd break her neck.

The tree stopped moving. The bracken was still. Why had I climbed in the first place? Why hadn't we just run home? Jo and her other worlds! She got me believing her fantasies and I always forgot she was making it up. I leaned back as much as I dared to glare at her.

The tallest branch was empty, leaves shimmering in the heat.

'Jo?'

She wasn't there. I'd imagined it all, running from that dog, from those boys, wishing I wasn't alone.

Suddenly, the bracken exploded. The dog came out with the last boy, threshing under thumps and kicks. A hand was over his muzzle and then released. All the dog's pent up fury exploded into vicious barking. Spittle flew. Shouting, the boys raced towards the tree, throwing stones.

'We know you're up there!'

I climbed higher until I was holding onto the slender highest branch. There was nothing over me but blue. I was higher than the mountains and as high as the distant larches.

'Psst,' said Jo.

I looked up and saw a door in the sky above my head.

'Catch hold,' Jo's hand appeared through the door, 'I was right! Come and see.'

And I reached up and wrapped my fingers round hers and let go of the tree, and the bullying world below faded away and I was Somewhere Else instead.

HEALER
Paula Harmon

I was only five when I found I could heal things. I picked up a butterfly, struggling to fly, its wings crushed by another child. My hand started to warm as I touched it and the butterfly lay still for a moment. I was sad, thinking it had died on my palm, but then it twitched and flapped its wings briefly before taking off into the sky. I didn't realise what I'd done then of course, I thought maybe it had revived with just the heat of my skin.

It probably wasn't until I was about twelve that the truth kicked in. My friend was in pain. Her stomach was hurting her. Cramps we thought. I tried to comfort her and she started to move away from me, but then she said 'your hands feel so warm – can't you put them on my stomach?'

It felt really weird, putting my hands on her like that – around the navel. You don't really touch each other that way, but she was beyond caring. For a while, she went from grey to green to white and her face contorted. I was scared – it didn't seem right to me. Then she relaxed and let out a sigh. With the sigh, her colour came back and my hand started to cool.

She turned to me and frowned: 'That was weird,' she said, 'I thought I was going to die – what did you do?'

'I don't know' I confessed, 'but maybe you should go to the doctor.'

We gave an edited version of events to her mother and she took her straight to A&E. Turned out she had acute appendicitis – the doctor couldn't believe it – said it had been about to burst and then seemed to heal itself just enough to get her to hospital in time.

It doesn't come all the time mind you, sometimes I can help someone with the pain or the stress, can help alleviate the depression on their mind and sometimes I can't. I never know when the gift will come, I just feel my hands warm up and realise that this is the time, this is the chance.

So what do I do now? This man in front of me – I know he's violent, a wife beater, bully – who knows what else. He is lying in agony in front of me, doubled up and my hands are glowing.

What do I do?

THE WEDDING GUEST
Val Portelli

It began at my best friend's wedding reception.

I saw him, thought "wow," and tried to catch his eye across the crowded dance floor, but lost sight of him amongst the throng of people. Disappointed, I got a little tipsy, flirted with Joe the best man, and even gave him my number to call me once I arrived home.

Several of us were staying overnight and there were a few bleary-eyed faces when we staggered down to breakfast the next morning. I hoped to catch sight of my mystery man in the dining room, but there was no sign of him. I tried to be subtle but a few of my friends teased me, although nobody seemed to know who he was.

Two weeks later Jackie returned from her honeymoon and we arranged to meet for lunch. Not surprisingly, when we met all she wanted to talk about was her new husband and show me the wedding photos. It was while we were browsing through them I saw right at the back, in one of the crowd scenes, a face I recognised.

'Who's that?' I asked, pointing him out. 'I remember seeing him at the wedding but he disappeared early.'

Jackie glanced where I was pointing then went very pale. 'I don't know,' she said, 'perhaps he was a friend of Dave's. Anyway, how about another drink?'

Even though our glasses were still half full she jumped up to go to the bar, and when she returned put away the album and started talking about how wonderful Jamaica was. I was sure she had deliberately changed the subject and wondered for a moment if he had been an old flame she didn't want to discuss.

For a while I didn't see much of her, and when I phoned she just made excuses about being busy. I knew she now had other commitments but couldn't help feeling hurt at the way she was cutting me out of her life. Apart from the occasional email, the next time I heard from her was an invitation to her baby-shower. All the gang would be there and I felt obliged to share in her celebrations. It was to be held in the same hotel where she had celebrated her wedding, and again several of us were staying overnight.

Although we helped to drink the bar dry, in view of her condition Jackie stuck to orange juice and retired early. The rest of us settled in for a good gossip in the cosy hotel lounge, and in our mellow state conversation turned to love lives, partners and plans for the future.

I had been seeing Joe regularly, but although he hinted at making it more serious, somehow for me the spark was not there. I enjoyed his company and his friendship, but it was the tall, dark-haired man I had seen at the wedding who haunted my dreams and fantasies. When the girls teased me about the next wedding being mine, I knew it was time to break up with him. I couldn't help noticing Penny's interest when I said we were just friends. It brought home to me that my life was a mess, and I needed to get out of the rut it had become.

At three in the morning, and slightly tipsy, we made our way back to our respective hotel rooms. I had only decided to attend at the last minute so wasn't in the main block with the others, but off a corridor in the annex, in the oldest part of the hotel. Bidding the others goodnight, I left the modern well-lit area and tried to remember the way back to my room. The archway almost hidden behind the old-fashioned fireplace looked familiar, and led me into a gloomy passageway, dimly lit by electric candles in old fashioned wall sconces. When I arrived all the connecting doorways had been open, but now I noticed signs saying "Fire exit" and the heavy oak partitions were firmly closed, invoking a peculiar feeling of claustrophobia.

It was also eerily silent, and for a moment I considered going back the way I had come, and asking someone from reception to point me in the right direction. Opening one last door, I breathed a sigh of relief when I saw a sign on the wall showing the direction to my room. Walking along a dead-end with my suite in sight, I jumped when I noticed a shadowy figure emerge from behind an aspidistra in a large pot at the far end of the corridor. The scream that rose in my throat died when I recognised the man I had been lusting over for months in my dreams.

'I knew you would come back,' he said in a deep sexy voice as I stood there gaping.

'Who are you?' I stuttered. 'What are you doing here?'

'My name is Adam,' he smiled, 'and I live here. Welcome back, Julia.'

'How do you know my name? You didn't even notice me at Jackie's wedding. What were you doing there anyway?'

'I attend all the weddings held here. You could say it's my job, has been for years.'

'You mean you're a waiter or something,' I asked, which brought a wry smile in response.

'Something like that. This was the home of my ancestors and I sort of stayed on when it was turned into a hotel. In fact, the room you have been allocated used to be my own chambers. You might have noticed this is the old part of the original building. Did you have a nice evening with your friend?'

'Yes, it was good. She seems very happy to be starting a family. Where were you earlier? I didn't see you.'

'Yes, it's a shame he's such a bullying shit who will treat her badly. Maybe it will be for the best when she loses the baby. I was there, I'm always there, but like a good waiter most of the time I'm invisible. I do what needs to be done and it's only a select few who actually notice me. That's why I couldn't acknowledge you at the wedding. I just had to wait until the right moment, and here we are.'

It was surreal and I wondered if I had drunk more than I thought. My hand was shaking so much I couldn't get the old-fashioned key in the lock, until Adam took it off me and easily opened the door, ushering me into the room. I was not surprised when he followed me in, although I noticed he left the key in the lock after he closed it behind us. I should have felt scared at this stranger intruding into my personal space, but for some reason I felt completely safe in his company.

Looking perfectly at home he made me a hot drink from the hospitality tray, strong black coffee, no sugar, exactly how I liked it, then accompanied it with a shot from the mini bar, before taking a seat on the sofa next to me.

'You know, Joe was never right for you. I'm glad you made the decision to end it. He and Penny will be celebrating their own wedding here next year. You were right to give them the opportunity to be together. In fifty years' time they will be back with their children and grandchildren to celebrate their Golden wedding anniversary.'

'And what about me? Where will I be in fifty years' time?' I asked quietly.

'Why, here with me of course, where you belong.'

I was too surprised to answer, but didn't resist when he gently pulled me into his arms and kissed me passionately. The rest of the night passed in a haze of love-making until I woke the next morning to find myself alone.

Perhaps too much drink and nostalgia had caused the erotic dream. Noticing the time, I showered and dressed quickly and made my way down to breakfast. The others were already there as I took the last remaining seat between Jackie and Penny. Neither was very talkative and it felt strange remembering what Adam had said about Jackie losing the baby, and Penny having a happy life with Joe.

I kept my thoughts to myself, and most of the girls assumed I was feeling fragile after drinking too much the night before. Once we had finished eating, we made our way back to our respective rooms to gather our things before meeting up in the foyer to say our goodbyes. The trip back along the corridors seemed quicker and much less daunting than it had the night before, although I hesitated outside the door to my room when I found it unlocked.

'Good Morning, Madam. I'm sorry. I thought you were still in the dining room. I can come back later to finish cleaning.'

'No, it's no problem. I've just come to collect my things then I'll be checking out.'

'If you're sure. I hope you slept well. It's a beautiful room isn't it, even if it is supposed to be haunted.'

'Yes, it's lovely. Who's supposed to haunt it?'

'Well, as you will have noticed, this room is part of the original hotel that dates back to the 17th century. The story goes that a tall, handsome man whose family owned the estate was betrothed to marry a beautiful local girl. On their wedding day his fiancée Julia never turned up, and he spent the rest of his days confined to the hotel unable to leave. Anyway, it makes for a good story. I hope we will see you again.'

'Yes, I'm sure you will. Thank you. Goodbye.'

Pulling my suitcase behind me I returned to the reception area deep in thought. There were the usual rounds of hugs and kisses and promises to keep in touch as everyone dispersed to catch their trains or taxis home. Penny pulled me to one side, and although hesitant to say what was on her mind eventually explained.

'Julia, did you mean it when you said you and Joe were only friends? I know he's very fond of you, and I wouldn't want to muscle in if you are serious about each other.'

'Go for it, Penny. He's a great bloke, just not for me. I'm sure you'll be very happy together. Don't forget to invite me to your Golden wedding.'

She blushed scarlet, then with another hug promised to keep in touch and left, leaving Jackie and me alone.

'I owe you an apology Julia. I know I've not been a very good friend since I got married, but things have been so complicated. It's been hard for Dave to give up his bachelor life-style, and now with the baby coming I haven't had much time for him. I always feel so tired and our sex life has become almost non-existent. I'm sure once she's born things will get back to normal and we'll be fine. Please forgive me and keep in touch. I really miss our girlie chats. Thanks so much for coming. It wouldn't have been the same without you here.'

With that she gave me another hug and went out to her waiting cab.

I felt a bit spooked. The conversations with my friends seemed to confirm everything Adam had said. Maybe he didn't really exist and my subconscious had just picked up the vibes from knowing my friends so well. Collecting my overnight bag I paid my bill, and made my way to the station to catch my train home. Work the next day went from bad to worse, and after a particularly nasty argument with my boss I plucked up courage and handed in my notice. Now I was committed and only had a month to find myself a new job.

The following week a major local employer unexpectedly went bankrupt, and the job centre was flooded with people looking for work. I was beginning to despair when I saw an agency advertising for a live-in administrator's position. At the same time my lease came up for review, and my landlady told me she needed my flat, as her niece was returning from Australia to live with her.

I contacted the agency, had the interview and got the job. Although I didn't know much about it the salary was good, the hours reasonable and it was in a town I knew about twenty miles away, so I accepted the offer there and then. A few days later I received the confirmation letter with full details. It was at the hotel where I had celebrated Jackie's wedding and baby shower. It seemed I would be returning sooner than I had expected.

Reporting for duty I was shown my office at the rear of reception, where I would be responsible for keeping the web site up to date, tracking logistics of visitors and assisting with the marketing of the hotel. Very occasionally I would be required to help out on the check-in desk but my hours would be nine to five, with Sundays and Thursdays free, meals provided and I would have my own private suite in the hotel. It was only when I was shown the same room where I had previously stayed that I had some second thoughts.

'They're lovely rooms,' the owner explained, 'but some guests feel uncomfortable being so far away from the main foyer. We decided the old part of the hotel would be allocated to staff, leaving the modern part for guests.'

Everyone was welcoming and helpful so I decided to make the best of it. I settled into my new home and always slept soundly, without any unwelcome intrusions. By Christmas, when I had been there three months, it had become my dream job. My marketing ideas were appreciated and implemented, and I was happy to see the occupancy rates steadily rising. The owners must have been pleased too, as my December pay packet included a handsome bonus, with a personal thank you for my contribution to the success of the hotel.

New Year's Eve we had our most successful party ever. Although it was hard work all the visitors enjoyed themselves, and the compliments came thick and fast from contented guests, with several enquiring about booking for the following year after having such a great time. At three in the morning I made my way back along the now familiar corridors, happy the evening had been such a success but ready for my bed.

I unlocked my door, still with the same old-fashioned key, only to be startled when a familiar sexy voice came out of the darkness.

'Welcome home, Darling Julia. A toast for a Happy New Year and our next fifty years together.'

With those few words my fate was sealed. As I raised my glass to his I knew my future had been preordained, and I would never be allowed to leave.

PATIENCE
Paula Harmon

She hobbled a little, the Old Woman. That's what they called her, the village children: The Old Woman. When she came to town to trade honey for cloth or flour, the nastier ones used to sneak into the store and while one of them distracted with tears or apparent shoplifting, one of the others would surreptitiously move the walking stick propped up on the counter. They would hide it in amongst a barrels of goods, or leave it outside the door. Once they put it in the horse trough. The Old Woman would limp round, her face grim with pain until she found it, then she would hobble to the edge of the woods. There she would turn around, her face still mostly hidden by her deep sided bonnet. She would stare at the village in silence. Somehow she always managed to be glaring exactly where the children were hiding.

No-one really knew how old she was or what she was called. People spoke hazily of a lost girl who appeared once but others thought they were muddling up forgotten fact with an old tale. The woman just kept herself to herself in the cottage in the woods, and for the most part seemed to have everything she needed apart from the means to make clothes or bread. The cottage was in a sunny dell where the trees surrounded as if encircling with a loving embrace but their branches did not spread too thickly overhead. She had a little garden, a huge beehive, a few grub-obsessed hens, a small bad-tempered goat and an even more bad-tempered goose. The children who tormented her in town rarely got close enough to torment her in the woods. A few stones were thrown sometimes, nasty dead things were left on the step at her gate but somehow whenever they did it, the trees seemed to rustle threateningly even though there was no wind and the hens would rush out to look for little grub-like toes and the goose would rush at them flapping her enormous wings and screaming. The goat, meanwhile, would eat anything they left, no matter how dead or how inedible and would glare at them with her demonic eyes until they backed away.

But the adults felt differently. When things went wrong: there was illness or fear, the adults would creep to the cottage at dusk and seek help. Sometimes as they approached, they overheard her talking to her bees and thought they'd heard her saying 'help him to find me'. It made them more nervous than ever to consult her and they tried to keep it from the priest, but in the end their need for healing was greater than their superstition, and somehow the woman's herbs and honey and listening ear seemed to resolve most things.

One summer evening, a stranger came to the town. He was riding on a beautiful horse, the like of which no-one had ever seen. The man looked wealthy but kind. He was old. Not very old perhaps, but slightly past his middle years. His face told of years of pain and hardship, despite his evident riches. When he stopped to rest the horse, he was offered a night at the inn but declined, saying bread and honey were all he needed and then he would be on his way. There was something sad and resigned in his face, as if he had travelled from disappointment to disappointment for many years.

The baker confessed he was out of bread and all the housewives too said that there was nothing left until tomorrow. The store keeper would have claimed the ownership of the best honey, but his supply had run out. There was nothing for it but to point him in the direction of the Old Woman.

The children followed discretely, wondering how the man would fare against the goat and the goose and the Old Woman's general disinclination for other people.

The man led his horse deeper into the wood until a swarm of bees surrounded him like a cloud. He stopped and the children hidden in the bracken, tensed, wondering what they would do if he was stung. But the bees just hovered round him, now more like a crown and their buzzing intensified. The man smiled. He straightened his back, calmed his horse and walked on.

From behind the trees, the children kept watch as he neared the cottage. In the twilight, they saw the Old Woman was at the gate. Not inside, but outside, a small bag at her side, as if she was ready to leave. Her bonnet hung from the hand holding the walking stick and her long hair flowed over her shoulders as if she was a girl. She was not really very old. Just past middle years. As the man approached she smiled. A deep beautiful smile. And she raised her face to him, holding his cheek with her other hand as she gazed into his eyes.

Gently he kissed her and briefly held her. Then he lifted her into the saddle and they followed the other path out through the woods and into the wide world.

DOOR BELLS
Val Portelli

There it was again. Someone ringing my doorbell at 3 a.m. At first I thought it was kids mucking about but surely they wouldn't be up at such an unearthly hour. Peering through the bedroom window I could see the outer front door, but there was no one there. After it happened a third time, always at the same hour, I decided to investigate. My research showed the wave lengths occasionally got mixed up, and someone at a nearby neighbour's door would make your bell ring instead of theirs.

Perhaps that was the explanation, although there was only one other home in the vicinity, and that was over a mile away, across the fields. By chance I met my nearest neighbour the following day in the village, while I was out shopping.

'Yes, I've heard of that before. When I lived in the cottage it nearly caused a riot between a few locals when it happened to them. Each blamed the other and it was only when one of them had their place rewired the truth came out. Mind you, I understand it has to be within a short distance, something like ten yards if I remember rightly, so it couldn't be mine. Anyway, I haven't got a doorbell, only my trusty old knocker.'

What were the other options? Could a bird or wild animal alight on the bell and accidentally set it off? Not possible, it was set within the enclosed porch and the timing was too consistent. It happened again the following night, and glancing at my alarm I saw it was exactly 3 a.m. I needed to get to the bottom of the mystery before it drove me insane.

The following evening, I prepared a thermos of hot coffee, turned out the lights, and settled down to read by the glow from my Kindle. Just before three I heard a noise, and grabbing the poker flung open both the inner and outer doors. The sound of the bell reverberated behind me but there was no one there. That's when I remembered the bell had been disconnected after the terrible accident when my partner had been electrocuted. He died at 3 a.m.

DO YOU HAVE ENOUGH TIME?
Paula Harmon

When I was little, my Uncle Edgar made a time-machine.

Most people would make one so they could go back and see Stonehenge built or go back to stop Dave from marrying that Nora. Or they'd go forward and get the lottery numbers.

But Uncle Edgar didn't.

His advert in the free paper said:

DO YOU HAVE ENOUGH TIME?
If not, call round to garage no 9
Willoughby Avenue
No charge. No catch.

Of course, aged five, I wasn't interested. For me, there was far too much time. Holidays and Christmas and birthdays and getting to be a big girl were all taking an age to arrive.

In fact, I never would have remembered about the time-machine if I hadn't found that box of newspapers in my parents' attic today.

Uncle Edgar nearly made the front page. But unexpected heavy rain meant the headline was 'April Showers Cause Car Chaos' rather than 'Local Man Makes Time Machine', which was on page two. Things soon changed.

The first customer was a student. With just one week to write his dissertation, he was desperate. With help from Uncle Edgar, he managed three months' work, several really good parties and a couple of brief romances in what was really just seven days.

Word spread. Young wives applied for more time to do housework (this was a long time ago you realise); couples applied for longer honeymoons; mothers asked for more time with their toddlers; people asked for time to sort out their incompetence before their bosses found out.

Uncle Edgar never asked a penny and everyone got exactly what they wanted. Yet it was all over in less than six months.

Reading the first article and seeing that long-forgotten face, I vaguely recall seeing him on some news programme in fuzzy black and white, in awe that someone I knew was on TV.

'I thought people would want time to change things, to heal things...' he kept saying.

'How do the requests seem to you, Mr Rudd?' asked the interviewer.

'Selfish,' sighed Uncle Edgar, 'just selfish.'

Flicking through the papers, I saw that the time-machine overtook politics, women's lib, hippies and fox-hunting as the top reason for writing to the editor.

'Sir, if I had paid any money, I would want it back. Something ought to be done about Mr Rudd. We have just returned from a week's holiday in Spain. We saved up all year. Mr Rudd turned one week into two months. Now no-one is speaking to anyone else and I have an appointment with the divorce lawyer on Monday.'

'Sir, an extra long honeymoon is a terrible thing. We ran out of things to say after six weeks and I've found out all his horrible habits. I wish I'd married the other bloke.'

'Sir, I wanted to be with my children thirty-six waking hours a day. I am now going grey and I am only twenty-four. Don't print my name. My husband always said they were little brats and I don't want him to know I now realise he's right.'

Only two letters stood out in praise.

'Sir, having spent a weekend away from 3b which Mr Rudd had extended to a month, I now realise what objectionable little toe-rags they are. I have handed in my notice and am off to work in a country where children prize their education.'

'Sir, I asked for extra time to improve my housewife skills. In the library looking for recipe books, I enrolled my husband on a cookery course while I learnt accountancy. We are both now much happier and about to open a hotel.'

But a final letter suggested sinister implications.

'Sir, are Mr Rudd's motives truly altruistic? Enemy agents are at this moment infiltrating our society with secret brain-washing machinery! How can we know that he is not central to this plot? All true Britons! For the sake of God, Queen and Country: boycott this fiendish device!'

Uncle Edgar closed down the garage in Willoughby Avenue.

I now live in a small town myself and know how scandals about nothing rumble round for what feels like forever and then blow over. In Uncle Edgar's case, the indignation about the time-machine was overtaken when the local chip shop started offering curry sauce and 'The Great Foreign Muck Food Poisoning' debate began.

I realise as I wade through the yellowed newsprint, that I last saw the time-machine in 1976. Uncle Edgar used bits of it to make me a radio which he put in a 1950s vanity case. Being an unconfident teenager, I didn't appreciate it. Already desperately uncool, I didn't want to be seen with something so old fashioned it probably couldn't pick up the 'right' station.

Putting the newspapers into a neat pile for recycling, I turn to the next set of things to sort. Deep in a battered cardboard box is the vanity case radio, covered in lovely cherry red leather. I am ashamed that I didn't thank Uncle Edgar enough and that I was more interested in other people's opinions than the work of art I possessed. Such is the regret of middle-age I suppose.

Clearing this attic is both sad and exhausting. I wish I could relish it more, that I didn't have to go back to work tomorrow, that most of this stuff will go to landfill because I only have today to go through it all.

I run my hands over the case and opening it, turn those solid dials which speak of a less disposable era. My fingers find something out of kilter, a little bit of imperfection. Tucked down between the radio and its case is a tiny slip of paper.

162

It reads, 'Dear Paula. Next to the left dial is a small button. One day, you'll want more time. If so, just press the button while you tune in. Make the most of it. Love Uncle E.'

With a trembling finger, I press….

GIGGLES IN THE NIGHT
Val Portelli

Even though my own kids were grown up and living away from home, I could still remember that feeling of trying to settle them at 3 a.m. when they wanted to play and I was in desperate need of sleep.

This was the third night in a row I had heard a child giggling in the early hours. The dividing wall between my house and my neighbour's was quite thick, and I had never been disturbed by sounds from next door before. The new owners were quite elderly but perhaps they had grandchildren staying. Maybe if it had been the TV or music playing, rather than a youngster's voice, I wouldn't have noticed it.

It was odd that I hadn't heard a sound during the day, only when I was working late at night on my manuscript. With a deadline looming I needed to get my latest novel finished and off to the publishers by the end of the week. Stretching, I stood up from my desk and wandered into the kitchen to make a hot drink.

The only noise in here was the tick-tock of the clock and the hiss of boiling water from the kettle. Going back into my office I realised the giggling had stopped. I worked steadily for a couple of hours, finally typed The End and with a sigh of relief took myself off to bed just as the birds started singing their little heads off to greet the new day.

With my manuscript winging its way to my editor I was able to resort to normal hours and even start tackling the garden, which had begun to look like a wild-life sanctuary.

'Good Morning. Beautiful day, isn't it?'

I looked up to find an elderly lady, secateurs in hand, and a basket full of weeds and dead flowers hanging over her arm.

'Yes, perfect,' I replied. 'I'm Jackie, and you must be my new neighbours.'

'Lovely to meet you Jackie. I'm Amy, and my husband George is skiving somewhere in his shed, pretending to be doing something useful to get out of the gardening.'

'Typical man,' I laughed. 'Are you settling in OK?'

'Yes, it's a lovely house. We were very lucky to find it, and at such a reasonable price too. Our old place was getting too big for us and only had a scrap of ground. I do love a garden and it's a lot closer to our grandchildren. I know we're going to be happy seeing out our days here.'

'I hope so. How many grandchildren have you got?'

'Four, and another on the way from our youngest. As soon as we get settled we're going to invite them over for a house-warming. Obviously, you and your husband will be invited. I'll let you know the details but we're thinking of having a barbecue in a couple of weeks' time, once the weather settles.'

'I'm a widow but that would be lovely; I'll look forward to it. Are any of your family staying with you at the moment? I thought I heard a baby laughing in the early hours this morning.'

Amy's face seemed to cloud over. 'No,' she said abruptly. 'Must get on,' and grabbing her basket she scurried away indoors.

Puzzled, I carried on attacking the weeds for a while until an elderly gentleman emerged from his shed and gave me a cheerful wave.

'Morning Love,' he called. 'Fancy tackling my weeds when you've finished with yours?'

'I thought that was Amy's domain, while you do important shed stuff,' I smiled.

'Shush, don't let her know I'm chatting up a lovely young woman instead of repairing the lawn mower or she'll have my guts for garters,' he laughed.

'George,' the voice came from the kitchen. 'Came you come in for a minute, please?'

'Too late, I've been rumbled. Catch you later love.'

I heard his voice asking cheerfully if the kettle was on before the back door was hastily slammed shut behind him. Maybe it was my imagination, but on the rare occasions I saw them over the following few days they seemed to be checking I wasn't in sight before scuttling quickly out of the house.

A week later I was getting out of the car, laden down with shopping bags, as they were returning home. George looked as if he was coming over to help when Amy noticed me and with a quick 'Good Afternoon' took his arm and almost dragged him indoors.

It was very odd as they had seemed so friendly at first, and I wondered if I had inadvertently done anything to upset them. The next day my manuscript came back from my editor and I resumed my late-night habits proofreading and amending. The first night was quiet and I was pleased with how much was achieved. Around 3 a.m. the following morning I stopped work to make myself a coffee and heard it again, the distinctive sound of a toddler giggling. Feeling like a snoop, I pressed my ear against the wall of the box room and discovered the sound was coming from the similar room on the other side. The houses were semi-detached and I visualised the child's room remembered from visits to the previous inhabitants.

Although we hadn't been particularly close they had showed me round their home, and their four-year-old had dragged me off to her bedroom to meet her dollies. Mandy was a sweet, cheerful child, always chatting and giggling and full of questions. Although her parents were rather an odd couple, it seemed strange she hadn't been in to say goodbye when they left. One day I had seen her in the garden playing tea-parties with her teddy, the next day the house was empty and the *For Sale* post had gone up.

There were often furtive visitors to the house in the early hours, and I wondered if there were drugs involved, or perhaps they had stopped paying the mortgage and done a moonlight flit. Shortly after their hasty departure I was away for a two-month book promotion tour, and when I returned the *For Sale* sign was gone, and there was evidence of new people moving in.

After our initial friendly meeting, I was disappointed Amy and George had been avoiding me, and was determined to find some way to restore harmonious relations. The opportunity presented itself when I finally completed my book and arranged a launch party and book signing in the community hall. The event had been well publicised in the local paper, and everywhere I went in the village posters advertised the event. Still, a personal invitation wouldn't hurt, and it would give me an opportunity to find out what had gone wrong.

'Hello. It's me, Jackie,' I called as I knocked on their door, flyer in hand. 'Anyone at home?'

No answer. Perhaps they were out or maybe just avoiding me. I knocked again and was just turning away when I thought I heard a faint shout 'Help.'

'Where are you? Are you alright?'

Silence, then almost a scream 'Up here, but for God's sake be careful.'

I recognised it as George's voice but he sounded scared out of his wits. Perhaps he had fallen and was lying helpless, unable to move. The front door was locked but then I heard another cry, 'Please, somebody help me.'

Rushing back into my own house I climbed the adjoining fence and pushed at their back door. It was open. It felt strange to be in a house so like my own but a mirror image. A resounding cry from upstairs made me forget all thoughts of intruding and had me dashing up the stairs towards the source of the noise.

Another scream, followed by a childish giggle pierced the silence as I headed towards the spare bedroom. Throwing open the door I stopped dead at the sight of George strapped to a chair and covered in blood.

My gasp of horror attracted the attention of the small child methodically stabbing him with a knife almost as big as herself. She turned as I approached and I recognised her as Mandy, but not the sweet little girl I knew before. Pure evil glared from her glazed eyes as I stood rooted to the spot.

'Run.' The weak shout from George brought me back to my senses as I fled down the stairs and garbled a message to the emergency services asking for help.

The story made front-page news for a few weeks, but the police refused to release any details. Local papers eventually settled on an elderly resident having a fall, and he and his wife moving into a retirement home as they were no longer able to cope on their own. The house went up for sale but remained empty.

My book was a great success and I was pressurised by my editor to get the follow-up out as soon as possible.

It's now 3.30 a.m. I yawn as I type The End on the first draft of my new novel. It's gone well and I'm looking forward to tackling the garden and clearing the long-neglected autumn leaves.

That's when I hear the giggling again.

A DRINK AT THE CROWN
Paula Harmon

Ann sips a sherry in the lounge bar of the Crown Hotel. Leaning against the panelled walls, she peers through the window, where leaves are falling into the gardens. Sighing, she places the glass on the window sill where the light can fall through it. The sherry looks like distilled autumn.

She had promised she would wait till he returned. But it has been a long wait. Picking the glass up, then putting it down again, she walks back to the fire and then out into the foyer. Looking up the stairs, she sees the whisk of black skirts and rolls her eyes. That woman is about again, poking her nose into the bedrooms, looking for someone who can talk to her. Best stay downstairs. He can't be much longer.

Back at the window sill, she looks past the staggering, swaggering man in the courtyard and beyond to the bridge over the Stour. There is a girl there, or perhaps a woman. Squinting, she shakes her head. Is the desperate creature really considering throwing herself in? To squander a precious life, what a terrible waste. If only she could...

The main doors open and a blast of cold damp air swirls in with a small group of people and though the room is already full, their entrance makes her turn round. She watches a man and two women find a table as a younger man approaches the bar and orders a pint

each of *Tanglefoot* and *Golden Champion* and two
glasses of dry white wine which he takes to the others.

Her hand on the sherry is shaking and she
tenses.

The older man takes a box from his pocket and
puts it on the table. The four people raise their glasses
in a toast.

'To Henry.'

'To Henry.'

She draws nearer and hovers behind the older
man.

'Go on Dad,' says the young woman, 'Open it.'

'It's a bit disrespectful,' admonishes the older
woman.

'Mum, what's disrespectful is that he was blown
to smithereens a hundred years ago and the only thing
they've found is a finger. And that finger and who
knows what else has been ploughed back into the
ground year after year until a few months ago.'

'I know but… it's a bit gruesome.'

'Mum, it's our great great grandpa. It's your
great grandpa. It's family. He'll be back under ground
later.'

Glancing at his wife, who shrugs and thins her
lips, the older man opens the box. The four people look
inside and tears are forming in their eyes.

But Ann doesn't notice them. She couldn't see
past them into the box if she wanted to but she does not
want to, because Henry is standing before her,
sweeping his cap from his head, bowing as if she was a
duchess and then sweeping her up in his arms. Just like

he always does. He has come back. Just like he promised he would. And tonight they will lie down together and sleep in peace.

YE OLDE TAVERN
Val Portelli

Exhausted, I tried to focus on the road ahead. The Satnav had packed up, I'd missed the turn-off and icy flakes were making the windscreen wipers work overtime. There must be somewhere in this God-forsaken place where I could rest for the night. As if I'd conjured it up, through the trees I caught a glimpse of flickering lights. Pulling into the overgrown parking area I sighed with relief as the door opened and I saw the welcome of a roaring log fire.

'Good evening, Sir. Looks as if it's a bit rough out. Was it just some ale you were after or a meal and room for the night?' the landlord asked as I approached the bar.

'All three would be good,' I said thankfully. 'I seem to have got lost so a night's sleep after a few beers, and some food would set me up perfectly to carry on tomorrow.'

'Not a problem. Room number 3 at the top of the stairs. Once you've freshened up, a pint and menu will be waiting.'

The large room was old-fashioned but clean, warm and with an enormous 4-poster bed complete with fresh-smelling sheets, blankets and a bedspread. After a quick wash I returned to the bar, supped a beer drawn from traditional pumps and ate a hearty meal of steak and kidney pie with all the trimmings, washed down with a few glasses of deep red wine. I was the only customer and it seemed churlish to refuse a final large brandy before retiring for a good night's sleep.

'It's odd how he reeks of booze, but there's not a pub within miles of here.'

The voice pounded through the fog of my brain as I regained consciousness to find myself lying in a ditch with my leg twisted at an unnatural angle beneath me.

A different voice. 'Combine drinking with travelling along these roads in a blizzard and what do you expect? Lucky for him we were passing or he could have frozen to death lying here all night.'

Another voice. I opened my eyes to see whitewashed walls, nurses in blue uniforms and a white-coated doctor standing over me.

'Where am I? How did I get here? I was asleep in the Inn.'

'You're in the hospital, my friend. Our ambulance found you when they were returning from an emergency. You'd crashed your car. Since the old Tavern closed fifty years ago the only drink you can buy is from the village shop, and that doesn't open on Sundays. Strange, our test didn't show any signs of concussion, but rest for a while and you'll be fine.'

It was only when I was discharged from the hospital a few days later that I discovered the receipt in my wallet.

Ye Olde Tavern.

Received with thanks the sum of one pound, seven and sixpence:

One room, one night, one guest.
One evening meal.
½ bottle of wine,
Two pints of Olde Beste.
Complementary brandy.
We hope you enjoyed your stay. Please call
again.
Dated: 25th November 1946.

QUIET COMPANY
Paula Harmon

I saw the household ghost yesterday evening.

During office hours, I working alone in the spare room, shuffling paper, tapping on a laptop, making calls.

Outside, in the winter garden, the courting pigeons shift and flutter on the fence, prospective lovers trying their chances and being dodged. A crow flies down. He flexes his wings in dismissal and the pigeons scatter. He raises his head and looks around in disdain, waiting till all eyes are on him. Then he lowers his beak, and with slow deliberation, sharpens it on the edge of the fence. Even the slinking cat bides her time, hiding in next door's cabbages. I may pause with a cup of tea to watch, then go back to work.

It has never felt lonely here. The ghost, a musical companionable presence, potters around. He plays the electric piano in the front room, wearing spectral headphones. All I can hear is the rhythm of thumping keys, which stop as I enter. He hums tunes from inside machines and knocks on radiators.

Sometimes there's a tap on the front door. I have to stop what I'm doing to go downstairs. Who's there? No-one. I imagine the ghost sniggering when he catches me out like that; his ghostly shoulders heaving noiselessly.

At night when the family is home, if I go to bed early, I can hear the ghost. He chats or sings with some other unbody. The voices are just too indistinct to understand and I know it's not the TV or radio downstairs.

Other times, he thumps about in the attic, rummaging through boxes.

'Go to sleep,' I tell him.

My husband mutters 'what?' then rolls over to snore.

No-one else ever hears the ghost. Until yesterday I had never seen him.

Recently, I've been so busy, I haven't stopped to chuckle or admonish him. I've been meeting deadlines, correcting drafts. Then I had to work away. In my hotel there was nothing to hear but city noises: buses, trains, strangers. Finally home, I went to bed too tired even to read, let alone feel charmed by voices from another world. Too tired to say 'hello'.

Then yesterday evening, I saw him. Through a gap in the hall curtains, night pressed against the glass. Then there was a flash of movement.

That's the ghost, I thought, *what's he doing outside?*

Today, I am alone in the house again. At first it was silent. Then the letter-box rattled. Now it's silent again.

Was the rattling from inside or outside?

Where is he? It is very quiet.

I am lonely.

I get up and start down the stairs. Will I find a real person outside? Has my ghost left?

There is no-one there. My shoulders relaxing, I bound up the stairs.

'Naughty ghost!' I admonish.

Suddenly syncopated rhythm rattles the pipes, the dishwasher croons and someone is playing hopscotch in the attic.

Shaking my head, I turn to my work again and smile, no longer alone.

Forgiven.

THINGS IN THE NIGHT
Val Portelli

What was that? Probably nothing, just me feeling spooked at being alone in the house. I was used to the bright lights of London, noise and movement at every turn, not being miles from anywhere with the nearest neighbour two miles away. A neighbour is someone who lives next door for goodness sake. I wouldn't have agreed to come but Adam had painted a picture of idyllic country life, rolling fields, fresh air, picturesque, friendly pubs and short drives to the beach on Sundays. Not quite the same hypothesis when I was sitting alone with no mobile signal or Internet access in a freezing room in the middle of January.

Damn him. OK it wasn't his fault he had been called back to London for a few days to sort out some work problems. He had assumed he would be able to run his IT business anywhere, and it had seemed a good idea at the time. It was only 9.30 in the evening, early by my standards, but peering through the curtains all I could see was blackness, not even a glimmer of a street light or car headlights. Although I never thought I'd say it, I'd give anything to hear the sound of an all-night party keeping me awake until the early hours. The TV was repeat of repeats; I'd read all my books and without Wi-Fi couldn't even pass the time on social media.

Something moved. Out of the corner of my eye I caught a glimpse of a shadow passing underneath the window. 'It's just a nocturnal animal out looking for something to eat,' I told myself as I hastily closed the curtains. Making a hot chocolate I tossed up between having an early night or being bored by the TV. Even going into the kitchen put my nerves on edge, even though every light in the house was blazing away. It gave me some comfort but was it actually advertising the fact that the premises were inhabited? The knock on the door made me jump. My hand was shaking so much I could hardly put on the safety chain.

'Hello. Who's there?'

Mistake. Now they knew someone was home and a woman at that. Why hadn't I just kept quiet and let them think the house was empty? Silence. My terror made my voice come out louder and angrier than I expected.

'State your business, or I'm phoning the police.'

Still no response. Going back to the window I peered through a crack in the curtains but the front door was too dark to see anything. I'd have to get Adam to put in a security light when he got back. Why was I thinking about mundane household things when I might be dead in my bed by the time he got home? Picking up the poker from the old-fashioned fireplace I took a deep breath, and opened the door a crack, making sure my weapon was in sight. No-one there. What should I do now? Take the chain off and confront them? Perhaps that's what they were waiting for. As I was standing there dithering the knock came again. The scream I emitted changed into an hysterical laugh as I realised the "knock" was a fox rummaging through my dustbin.

After a quick glare at me for disturbing his feast he took off into the darkness.

I needed to get a life and stop being so neurotic. Closing and double locking the door I decided it was time to learn the country ways. Early to bed, early to rise and all that. Tomorrow I would go for a long walk into the nearest village, get to know my neighbours and become integrated into country life. There were bound to be activities organised by the local WI in the village hall, and knowing there was someone I could phone who wasn't hundreds of miles away would help me feel less alone.

Time for bed, even if it was only just gone ten o'clock. Even after going round all the house checking the windows were locked, I realised I was scared to go upstairs. Making as much noise as possible I stomped up the steps, checked all the rooms then feeling satisfied went back down to fetch a glass of water. That's when I noticed the back door was open. Had I forgotten to close it? Was there someone in the house?

I was still holding the poker but grabbed the large kitchen cleaver to add to my armoury. The sudden noise of someone moving in the lounge caught my attention. For a few seconds I dithered then came to my senses, slammed and locked the back door and crept towards the gloom of the front room. There was someone in there, bending over the sideboard. I tried to flick the light switch but nothing happened, the room stayed in darkness. The intruder half turned as I rushed towards him, and more by luck than judgement I connected and drove the knife into his torso.

A gargled scream left his throat as he collapsed to the floor while I rushed to find a torch, and grabbing my mobile frantically phoned for the police. By some miracle the connection had been restored and I was able to give my address and describe what had happened as I pleaded for help. The prowler hadn't moved when less than ten minutes later two officers appeared and took control. I saw one shake his head at the other, even as he called for an ambulance.

'So that's my story your Honour. I wasn't to know Adam was worried when he couldn't get me on the phone and had decided to come home early. He couldn't use his key because of the chain on the door so had checked out the back way rather than scare me. I never meant to kill him. If only he'd called my name I would have known who it was.

NIGHT-STALKER
Paula Harmon

You will say that it was in my imagination, worsened
by the fear in London at that time. You realise that
well-bred ladies were neither deaf, nor incapable of
reading the servants' papers in November 1888, and so
you attribute my story to the assumption I had absorbed
the hysteria over those poor unfortunate butchered
women.

But what happened was nothing to do with illicit
reading of the Illustrated Police News. Neither was it all
in my mind, although my mind was sorely troubled
then. 'Why troubled?' you ask. Ah, you see my
husband William had stopped loving me and had
abandoned my bedchamber for his own. And I realised
he was betraying me.

So that is when it started.

Has this ever been your experience? Daylight
drained me, night tormented me: my soft pillows were
leaden, each ticking second was a needle in my
whirling mind. When finally I slept, nightmares took
possession: I was in a carriage racing who knows where
and it was icy and raining, the lights dimming and the
carriage out of control, and I looked out of the window
and realised there was no driver and no means of
stopping…. or sometimes… if I described them you
wouldn't understand - images: a swirl of darkening
colours drawing me in, a man looking out of the

shadows brandishing a spoon, castles appearing, forming and reforming in the wallpaper and all along the belief I was awake. And finally when day came, I was too exhausted to rise.

One morning, the maid drew back the curtains and I looked out onto a fog which was sneaking through the window frame and seemed to be reaching out to envelop me. I could think of nothing I would prefer than being lost in it forever. I rose, left the children in the care of Nanny and taking the maid sought a pharmacy some way away. Yes, we were fearful, but I felt I could endure my malady no longer and we were, of course, not in Whitechapel.

I found an old fashioned place which appeared to have no gas supply. The gloomy oak interior was lit with candles, struggling in vain to illuminate a shop darkened further by the lack of light coming from outside. I explained my desperation to the chemist: my sleeplessness, my exhaustion, my malaise, my nightmares. He listened attentively, his features melting and reforming in the flicker of the candlelight, asking few questions and nodding sagely. Eventually he retreated into a back room, and just when I thought he must have forgotten me, he returned with a blue glass bottle, heavily ribbed, a fresh cork sealed with black wax.

'Follow the dosage,' he advised, 'It is an old remedy and you must take it sparingly.'

I read the script written on the label and for three nights I followed the instructions by the letter, but it seemed to have no effect. On the fourth, I doubled the dosage and fell into a fitful sleep almost immediately. Past midnight, the waking nightmare returned. To my terror I saw a man at the foot of the bed closing up a small bag and smirking. There was a miasma around me but I could see him through it - a sharply dressed man, with elven, almost devilish features. At that moment, he looked up and saw me watching him. I cringed back but then realised my shock was reflected in his face. Frowning, he sprang for the door and passed through without opening it. At the same moment, I realised I was not dreaming but wide awake.

I do not know what came over me. Fury I suppose, had been building for some time. I got up and opening the door, followed him - I could see him springing down the stairs and hampered by my nightgown could barely keep up. He passed through the closed front door as I reached the bottom step. I stood there hesitating. Should I open the door and pursue him? Hardly. Should I open the door and shout for a policeman? And tell him what? Should I go and rouse my husband? In the seconds I considered this, the door opened and my husband himself came in and the clock struck two.

'Amelia!' he exclaimed, 'What are you doing?'

'I thought I heard an intruder,' I answered, 'and I thought you were in your bed. Where have you been?'

'You needn't concern yourself with that,' he answered, bolting the door behind him. 'Now go back to bed.'

'Did you see a man outside?'

'Don't be foolish. Go back to bed. You will catch your death.' He didn't sound as if that would displease him, but I went.

The following evening I increased the dose again. Sleep came but no nightmares. However I woke after midnight again and feeling uneasy, got up and looked out into the street. Night after night the same.

In the end I could not bear feeling imprisoned by trying to sleep and took to creeping out to walk the streets, dressed up in my husband's clothes, keeping my head ducked down like all the other men.

It was another world, the soft puddles of yellow under the gas lights, the glimmer in the puddles, the unknown others going about unknown business. And how wonderful to stride and breathe deep, unencumbered by skirts and corsets, my hair rolled up under the top hat, my hands deep in the coat pockets. The air was pungent with coal smoke and horse dung and straying from home, pungent with people too: tobacco, alcohol, sweat. Women appeared and ventured forward but I kept to the shadows away from them, peering back in fascination: their finery a little out of date and grubby, their faces too red - not always paint but ill health too. Unobserved, they lolled, bored and gossiping, but observed they coquetted and simpered. If the man passed, they slumped again, pulling their darned silk shawls around them. If he didn't, they went off with him into the shadows. When one departed, the other women peered after her, piercing the man's back with their memories, fear under painted smiles.

Then one night I saw the intruder again, springing down the road. He was still carrying a bag in his gloved hand and he was springing up steps, disappearing through closed doors and moments later reappearing through the door and springing further down the road, his bag lighter, his grin broader. And I realised that no-one but I could see him. He bounced past the tawdry women, past the slithering men, through them, springing over them; invisible and unheard.

Eventually I managed to confront him, catching him by his arm as he emerged from a house.

'Who are you?' I whispered.

He twisted in my grasp and leaned down to stare into my face. His nose was inches from mine. His mouth was grinning but his eyes glinted. His pointed teeth were yellow and his breath sulfurous.

'I am Nightmare,' he hissed, and wrenched himself from my grasp. Something fell from his bag as he bounded away - a small glittering ball. It rolled and sparkled towards an exhausted street walker who was slumped in a doorway and hitting her foot, broke open. A glistening miasma engulfed her and after a moment she started to twitch, then she started to shudder and then she screamed herself awake.

Shaken, I went home. The following day I took the maid and tried to find the pharmacy who had sold the sleeping draught, but we must have mistaken our way because it could not be found and I have not found it since.

After that, I continued to take the dose but remained indoors and resolutely stayed in bed with my eyes closed until morning, even if I was awake.

Until that night.

That night I awoke, my heart thumping in my throat and overwhelmed with a sense of foreboding. I rose and left my room and crept to William's chamber. Opening the door, I saw him fast asleep in his bed, murmuring quietly in his sleep. Walking over to his side, I looked down on him and at that moment, a movement made me turn and I saw Nightmare at the foot of the bed, opening his bag and leering.

I recalled loving my husband so much once. I remembered smoothing his face as he slept, his arms holding me close, his head on my breast. I tried to remember when the love had soured and wondered if there was any hope of reviving it. I rushed at Nightmare and tried to clasp the bag shut but he pulled his arm from me. As we struggled, the bag burst open and a thousand balls flew into the air and crashed down onto William, exploding as they struck him.

William sat up, his eyes opened wide in terror. Whatever he saw made him flail, and then his mouth opened in a soundless scream before he fell back, horror still frozen on his lifeless face.

Nightmare threw his head back and breathed in the terror-filled miasma. Then, cackling with laughter, he disappeared.

The doctor said it was a stroke, unusual for a man of William's age but implied that habits of which I was ignorant might have led to it.

And I am here doctor, begging you for help. Because all I can hear, as I toss and turn in my bed, are the last words Nightmare hissed as he left: 'Murderer - you killed him - and now you will never sleep again.'

ABOUT PAULA HARMON

Paula Harmon has lived in Dorset since 2005. She writes chiefly but not entirely in the historical mystery genre but has a soft spot for the things that can't be explained and has been waiting to meet a dragon since childhood. So far, she's only met the human kind, but there's plenty of time.

https://paulaharmon.com
viewauthor.at/PHAuthorpage
https://www.facebook.com/pg/paulaharmonwrites
https://www.goodreads.com/paula_harmon
https://twitter.com/Paula_S_Harmon

To get news about my books and others, as well as the first chance to read Advanced Reader Copies of any new releases, please sign up for my newsletter at
https://paulaharmon.com/newsletter/

THE MURDER BRITANNICA SERIES (2nd Century Roman-Britain)
Murder Britannica
Murder Durnovaria
Murder Saturnalia

THE MARGARET DEMERAY SERIES (1910s London)
The Wrong Sort To Die

THE CASTER AND FLEET SERIES
(series with Liz Hedgecock set in 1890s)
The Case of the Black Tulips
The Case of the Runaway Client
The Case of the Deceased Clerk
The Case of the Masquerade Mob
The Case of the Fateful Legacy
The Case of the Crystal Kisses
The Case of the Peculiar Pantomime

OTHER BOOKS
The Good Wife (novella)
The Cluttering Discombobulator (memoir)
Kindling (short stories)
The Advent Calendar (short stories)
An Invitation for Christmas (short stories)
The Quest (novella)
The Seaside Dragon (for 7-11 year olds)
Weird and Peculiar Tales (with Val Portelli - short stories)

ABOUT VAL PORTELLI

Val was nine when she received her first rejection letter from a well-known women's magazine. Undeterred, she carried on writing for pleasure until a freak accident left her house-bound. To save her sanity she put fingers to laptop resulting in her first novel being traditionally published in 2013. A second book through different publishers increased her knowledge of how things worked, and she progressed to self-publishing, migrating from her original pen name of 'Voinks' along the way.

She writes in various genres, including short stories which often reveal her trademark 'Quirky' twist, and finds a constant source of inspiration from everyday events and passing comments. Several stories have been included in published anthologies, and some are now available in audio format under the 'Val's Tales' insignia. Two new books are underway, and will be completed once she stops procrastinating.

Reviews are always appreciated, as they help buy food for the Unicorns she breeds in her spare time.

To find out more, please visit
https://voinks.wordpress.com/about/

BOOKS BY VAL PORTELLI

ABC Destiny
https://mybook.to/ABCDestiny
Three girls from very different backgrounds, a woman alone, a male on a mission involving a disreputable older man. How are their lives entwined? Kismet has a way of revealing the ties that bind.

Alderslay
https://mybook.to/Alderslay
An old house. A new start. Ancient secrets.

What is the connection between Gina and the dilapidated mansion she hopes to share with her fiancé Paul? Is he committed to the renovation project or is local businessman Steve more likely to have the support of the reticent local villagers?

As uncanny coincidences link Gina to the gruesome history of the house, she must decide where her future lies, and if she is prepared to pay the final price.

Listen to Love
https://mybook.to/ListentoLove
A collection of short stories with Love as their theme, but be prepared for some surprises. Dementia, ghosts, murder, jealousy, second chances and even inanimate objects all find their place. Before each story is a brief introduction,

giving the background and inspiration. Many were inspired by song titles, but the stories are as varied as Love itself.

Spirit of Technology
https://mybook.to/SpiritofTechnology
What lies beyond the ether? An email from an unknown source, a developing relationship but should she trust her instincts or is she being stalked? A surprising ending which might or might not be factual.

Story of a Country Boy
https://mybook.to/StoryofaCountryBoy
The story of TJ, a brash, illiterate teenager, desperate to escape the confines and restrictions of his impoverished Mediterranean village. His journey leads him through the sleazy side of 1960s Soho, and opens his eyes to a different world as he seeks to achieve his dreams.

With each re-telling, the legend evolves.

Summer Changes Winter Tears
(Originally published as Changes)
https://mybook.to/SummerChangesEBook
A series of unexpected events encourage Zoe to adopt a new persona and leave dull and rainy London for an extended holiday in the sun. Life on the Mediterranean island of Malta is idyllic, especially when Reno appears on the scene, and she determines to settle there permanently.

A family emergency has her rushing back to her childhood home, and having to decide where her heart truly lies.

Changes trailer
https://www.youtube.com/watch?v=UqXmxSrZsxo

Weird and Peculiar Tales (with Paula Harmon)
https://mybook.to/WeirdandPeculiarTales

Anthologies

Flashpoint
The book of Books
The Wordsmith Chronicles
When Stars will shine
(A charity anthology of short stories in aid of Help For Heroes.)

Amazon author page:
https://author.to/ValPortelli

Facebook:
www.facebook.com/ValsTales

Blog:
www.Voinks.wordpress.com
Newsletter sign-up
https://Voinks.wordpress.com/sign-up
To find out more, please visit
About me – The person behind the page – Voinks
(wordpress.com)

Publishing website
www.quirkyunicornbooks.wordpress.com

Goodreads:
https://www.goodreads.com/wwwgoodreadscomVal_Porte
lli

Twitter:
https://twitter.com/ValPortelli

Val's Tales:

YouTube
www.youtube.com/channel/UCsmbM57q4SzHbOcx3C
Pbr1Q
Twitter:

https://twitter.com/vals_tales

Instagram

https://www.instagram.com/vals_tales

For availability options and to be kept up to date with future books by these authors please contact them via their individual websites or visit **www.QuirkyUnicornBooks.wordpress.com**

Reviews

If you enjoyed this book PLEASE consider leaving a review.
Leaving an Amazon review is like telling your friends how much you enjoyed a book.

Did you know you don't have to have purchased the book through Amazon to be able to leave a review there?
Reviews don't have to be complicated. The number of reviews is important so just a few words will be fine.
5 reviews will buy 1 ounce of fairy dust.
10 reviews will feed a Unicorn for a week.

50 reviews on Amazon will bring the book to the attention of a wider audience.
100 reviews provide the authors with the magic key to other worlds so they can write more stories for your enjoyment.

On behalf of mystical creatures and authors everywhere, Thank You.

Printed in Great Britain
by Amazon

70479594R00123